GLORY

TIMBER-GHOST, MONTANA CHAPTER

DEVIL'S HANDMAIDENS MC
BOOK 5

D.M. EARL

© Copyright 2023 D.M. Earl
All rights reserved.
Cover by Drue Hoffman, Buoni Amici Press
Editing by Karen Hrdlicka
Proofread by Joanne Thompson

All rights reserved. No part of this book may be reproduced in any form or by any electronic or mechanical means, including information storage and retrieval systems—except in the case of brief quotations embodied in critical articles or reviews—without permission in writing from the author.

This book is a work of fiction. The names, characters, and places portrayed in this book are entirely products of the author's imagination or used fictitiously. Any resemblance to actual events, locales, or persons, living or dead, is entirely coincidental and not intended by the author.

The unauthorized reproduction or distribution of this copyrighted work is illegal. Criminal copyright infringement, including infringement without monetary gain, is investigated by the FBI and is punishable by up to five years in federal prison and a fine of $250,000.

If you find any eBooks being sold or shared illegally, please contact the author at dm@dmearl.com.

ACKNOWLEDGMENTS

Karen Hrdlicka and **Joanne Thompson** my editing and proofreading team. I'm beyond blessed to be working with these two ladies. Between them Karen and Joanne polish my stories so they can shine. With their eyes on my stories I feel you're getting the best book it can be due to their experience and knowledge of how I write.

Debra Presley and **Drue Hoffman** @ **Buoni Amici Press**. Talk about being on top of everything. My two publicists work endlessly to handle the social media aspect, formatting, publishing and so much more which allows me to concentrate on my writing. They are awesome angels and I'm thrilled to have them be part of my team.

Enticing Journey Promotions and **Itsy-Bitsy Book Bits**. These two promotional companies help me with every new release and are very professional and always on top of everything.

Bloggers every single one of you. What you do for each and every one of my stories I can never repay you. Please know how much I appreciate each share, mention, post, and video.

My **DM's Babes** (ARC Team) and **DM's Horde** (Reader's group). These women in these two groups have become part of my family. I'm thrilled to spend time and engage with each and every one of them.

READERS without each of Y'all I'd not be able to live out my life's dream of writing books that make people tingle and just feel deep in their souls. Your support fills my heart and feeds my soul.

ANDIE RHODES special thanks sistah for letting me use your Devil's Handmaidens Motorcycle chapter in Glory's story. I appreciate Harlow, Peppermint and Momma being there for Glory and all abused women on the East Coast. I so appreciate you.

ONE
'GLORY'
NORA

Knowing Olivia is safe and being watched at Tank and Momma Diane's house enables me to be right where I couldn't wait to be. With my Boo after this long as fuck trip to rescue Vixen's friend and bring that asshole Juice down. Though now we have so many souls depending on us, it's going to take our village within the Devil's Handmaidens, along with everyone else we know. But that is for tomorrow, tonight is for us.

"Bae, what's put that look on your beautiful face? You should be on top of the moon since not only did you save Poodles but all the other women and all those babies. My God, what kind of deviant motherfucker does what Juice did? Talk to me, Glory girl, that's why I'm here."

"Awe, Boo, I'm sorry. This is the drop I get after every goddamn mission when I get home. It's like everything hits me at once and the emotional swing is just plain exhausting. It's not you, swear to Christ. If I'm honest here, when I had a moment to think, you were always on my mind. I was beyond thrilled when our convoy was riding in and I saw you on guard duty, though wish I could have jumped out and ran into your arms."

"Well, now for my honesty, kinda blew my mind when I saw that little one wrapped around you. How'd that happen?"

Watching his face, I can't tell if he's just curious or if he's just not that into kids. If it's the first cool, but if it's the latter then we have a huge problem. Been there, could have written the book on a guy not into kids, but to this day it's too fucking painful. Better to find out now than waiting and ending up in a mess of pain.

"So you asking, Boo, 'cause you don't like kids or just because you're curious how Olivia ended up coming back with me?"

He jumps out of bed and immediately starts pacing back and forth like a, I don't know, lunatic or psycho, pick one as I watch the shitshow in front of me.

"Really, Nora? I can't believe you just asked me that. I do a ton of shit with kids all the time. And I'm probably one of the closest to lil' Teddy. What is up with you tonight? If you didn't want me to stop by should have just said it, instead of trying to pick a fight with me when I'm just trying to be here for you. I've been totally honest with you about everything. Told you to ask me anything you want to know about and I've answered honestly, no matter how personal or brutal some of your questions were. But I get it, honestly, especially after you shared what happened in New Jersey and New York. I'm not one of those Italian mafia pricks you're used to, apparently. No, don't get all pissed off now, Nora, you started this shit with the asinine kid questions. Have I ever made you feel like I didn't like kids or wouldn't want them around? The answer is a big fat fuckin' NO."

Knowing I'm being a total bitch, I get out of bed and when he turns and stalks toward me, I grab him, pulling tightly so I can hold on to him. At first he puts up a weak struggle, but eventually he gives in.

"Boo, I'm sorry for being a major bitch. What Olivia told us has me wanting to go out and castrate every deviant out there in the world. She's a little fucking kid, for Christ's sake. That asshole, Juice, altered her life path and it will never be the same, no matter what happens going forward. That is what is killing me. I hate that we didn't rescue her before anyone of those dicks from the Thunder Cloud Knuckle Brotherhood or Juice and his degenerate lowlifes put their eyes and hands on a little innocent girl, after they murdered her parents right in front of her. Maybe I was looking to fight with you because I'm so goddamn mad, and I can't change a single thing for Olivia."

He wraps me up in his strong arms, resting his chin on the top of my head. Whispering, he tells me to breathe deeply and I listen and do it.

"Bae, you've already changed shit for that little girl. You saved her, Nora. Imagine if you hadn't gone and no one checked that room. Who the fuck puts a live child in a room with dead ones? For every evil that has been done to that child, you are already replacing those deeds with good ones. You and your club, Tank and Momma Diane, Ollie and his folks, will all come in contact with your lil' Olivia and will help you change the direction her life is going. Now she will have so many choices it will seem like the sky's the limit. Don't beat yourself up, babe, please. Hey, if you're worried about her, I can drive you over to Tank's right now so you can check on her. Is that what you want, Bae?"

Shaking my head right before tears start rolling down my cheeks, it hits me how much I care for this man in my arms. He's the exact opposite of what I grew up with and closer to who I hooked my star to all those years ago. Before the psychopath changed my life forever.

"No, don't want to go there but if you don't mind, I'm going to call Vixen to make sure she's all right. It won't take but a minute or two, promise."

He turns me around and places a whisper of a kiss on my nose before leaning into me so his forehead is touching mine. His eyes are intently watching me, and I can see the multitude of colors in his gorgeous eyes.

"Nora, do what you have to. I'm going to go down and grab some snacks, then I'll be back. Glad we were able to talk this through. If we do this, then we'll never have problems. You want anything in particular? And don't worry, I'll be careful and stealth-like so no one will see me."

Shaking my head, I watch him pull on his jeans and T-shirt, along with sliding his feet into his boots without socks, and he heads out of my room quietly, slipping into the hallway. Grabbing my phone, I dial Vixen and she answers on the first ring.

"Well shit, sister, took you long enough. Taz won the bet on how long before you called to check on your girl. Anyway, she's out like a light, holding on to her new bear Momma Diane bought her. She seemed to have a blast with Declan, Amelia, and her boyfriend, Teddy. Damn, Glory, they are so frigging cute together. He must watch Enforcer with me because he held the door for her when they were done playing outside with the dogs. Then he shared his throw when they were watching the movie she picked out. When it was time for bed, as they were all getting ready, he leaned over and told her how much fun he had and wished her sweet dreams. Then she gave him a hug. Glory, I thought Taz was going to lose it and Enforcer wasn't that far behind. Teddy, who isn't into that touchy feely shit, gave your girl a hug right back. So all in all, everything is great. Oh, before anyone else can tell you, I'm engaged and I'm pregnant. Night."

Before I can say a word, the phone goes dead. Holy mother of God, Vixen is engaged and pregnant all at the same time. It takes me a minute, but I text her congratulations on both just as my door opens and he comes in, arms full of goodies on a tray of some sort.

"Everything okay with the kids?"

"Yeah, and Vixen is engaged and knocked up. What a way to end a night, I guess."

"Wait, what? How did she get engaged and pregnant

since we saw them last? Damn, Ironside works fast. Well, good for them. Personally, I'm thrilled to see it working out for them since it sounds like they've been to hell and back. Now, are you hungry, Bae?"

My eyes take him in from the top of his head with that long wavy hair to his beautiful, sculptured face, broad shoulders, ripped chest and abs, down to his thick thighs, and as my eyes watch, a thickening and bulging crotch. Smiling and licking my lips, I don't answer him in words.

"Well, thank God you have a fridge. Let me put this shit away and I'll be right there."

Laughing, I make my way to the bed, lounging in it for maybe a minute before he's all over me with those full, firm lips of his. Hearing his deep throaty growl as he literally devours my moans, *it might be time to let this secret out of the bag before any other female gets any ideas about this sensational man about to give me my third, no, fourth orgasm of the night.*

That's my last thought until after my final one which we shared, then he finally cuddles up close, his nose in my hair while my fingers are clutched to his as I drift to sleep surrounded by all that is him, my Boo.

TWO
'???'
BOO

Watching Nora sleep has become one of my favorite things to do. She tries to have this tough, silent kind of persona, but when you get to truly know her you realize that's all an act so she can protect herself. Now, the question is from what.

She's given me very little of her background and past. I know she came from a Devil's Handmaidens chapter somewhere in New Jersey. And her family is out East and she talks to them here and there. The few times I've brought them up she immediately shut down. So even without words that tells me a lot.

Though that thought also hits me in the gut 'cause I've not been upfront and honest with my Bae either. I mean my family is fucked up for sure, but a normal messed the hell up. It's from when I joined the service and all I did over there. That is what fried my head. If not for what I do now, I'd probably be one of the statistics of twenty-two a day, which means at least twenty-two veterans every day take their own lives.

Right now, the only time my nightmares stay away is when I'm next to this woman. Something about her keeps my demons away. And that shocks the ever-lovin' fuck outta me 'cause I've spent time with women over the years since I came stateside, but not one has been like Nora.

Feeling her body tense then relax I know one of her dreams is turning into a nightmare. Unfortunately, I don't keep all of hers away. Nora did share one night that until I came into her life, she had nightmares every night, so she would take all the graveyard shifts and duties within her club as she couldn't get a good night's sleep. As I feel her relax against me again, my mind wanders. We have a good thing going on, but we're pressing our luck. Don't know how many goddamn times we almost got caught. Not sure why we're sneaking around like snot-nose teenagers, for Christ's sake. She's a badass Devil's Handmaidens sister and I fought overseas in wars and did things that if anyone knew about, it would shock the hell out of the folks here in the States.

Needing to pee, I get up and walk to the en suite which is tits. My God, Tink spared no expense. Just when I'm about done I hear the tap-tap-tap before the bedroom door opens. *Motherfucker*, I think to myself. I'm not sure who's coming into Glory's room, but I can't get caught here. Putting the lid down without flushing, I step into the walk-in closet, going to the farthest corner I can. Not gonna hide behind my woman's clothes unless I have to. Then I hear Nora's voice and she sounds pissed.

"What the fuck are you doing in my room? Yeah, I'm sleeping. What did you expect, that I'd be swinging from the ceiling fan? Jesus Christ, don't you ever give up? NO, there is no one here with me. Do you see anyone?"

"Why's the bathroom door closed then, Glory?"

"Not that it's any of your business, sister, but had a stomach issue and closed the door to keep the stench out of my bedroom. Anything else you want to ask me? Maybe what I ate for dinner, or the last time I blew a guy and swallowed?"

"Well, that's kind of strange you would throw that in there, Glory. Why do you have bjs on the brain? Maybe because you've been busy with your mystery meat."

"That's it, get the fuck out, Raven. No, I've had enough. Move your ass and walk out the door before I literally carry you, you mouthy lil' shit, out. NO more, hear me! My personal life is just that, personal and private. If I want to share shit with you that's great but until then got nothing for you, so leave. What the hell are you doing? Get out of there, you have no business in there. For Christ's sake."

I hear the bathroom door open and someone walk in. That's when I chicken out and climb behind Glory's clothes. I carefully shift my feet under her shoes on the floor and make sure I slow my breathing. I can hear from what Nora called out, her sister Raven is moving around and even hear the shower door open and close.

Right as she enters the walk-in closet, I hear an *ump*, then a garbled, "Holy shit, what the fuck, Glory? I'm only playing with you. God, you go from nothing to absolutely fuckin' crazy lunatic in one point one seconds. I'm outta here."

Not moving and barely breathing, I stay exactly where I'm at, even after the door closes. I hear Nora looking around before she comes into the closet. She sniffs the room then giggles softly. Standing in the middle of the room, I hear the light go on and when I barely shift, I see her grinning like a loon.

"Come out, come out, wherever you are, Boo. Coast is clear."

I shift the clothes out of the way and step past the mess on the floor. That surprises me and not in a bad way. Glory is neat as can be but now seeing her closet floor, I feel better. I keep shit tidy and in place but I'm not a fanatic with dusting and vacuuming at all.

"What the hell was that about, Bae? Does Raven know something or just thinks she has a clue?"

"Shit, I don't know. Remember when Taz had her nightmares back a few months ago? That was when you got back in town so I had on that pastel pink nightie. Well, didn't think about it and ran out of here like the hounds of hell were chasing me. When I got to Taz's room and everything calmed down, Raven caught what I was wearing and almost came back to the room. That would have been a surprise. You in my bed, all that hair, with your ripped body. Not to mention I left you tenting the sheets. Her mouth would have fallen open and those eyes would have literally popped outta her nosy head. She's starting to piss me off. Sorry 'bout that."

I pull her close, covering her open mouth with mine. I start slow but work my lips to the way I like it, rough. Glory whimpers but doesn't push me away, so I lean down and pick her up in my arms.

"Don't, put me down, Boo, you're gonna drop your balls, for Christ's sake. I'm not a lightweight like Tink and Peanut. Come on, if you hurt yourself then we won't be able to finish what we're starting."

Ignoring her pleas, I walk to the bed with the most intriguing woman I've ever met in my arms, my mouth on hers. When I go to lift my mouth, hers follows like she doesn't want me to leave. That brings a smirk to my face. I place Nora on the bed, immediately pulling her down to the edge. I plant myself between her spread legs. Leaning forward, I pull at her panties but don't rip them. Not anymore, once she told me what she paid for these beauties. I still grab at them but instead of ripping them off, I pull them down her legs.

When she's bare, I can smell her excitement, which gets me harder than I was a second ago. I take my tongue to her inner thighs, licking upward but not going anywhere near where she wants me to go. Nora is beside herself, begging me to put my mouth on her. Her moans and soft screeches are driving me crazy. When I move farther up between her legs and separate her intimate lips, I blow softly and she literally levitates from her hips down. Not able to tease her any longer, I open my mouth, suck in her clit, then bite down. Her body tenses all over before she floods my face and her body shakes uncontrollably. I don't stop my sexual advances on her body until she once again begs me, but for an entirely different reason… to get me to stop this time.

Standing up, I reach for my boxer briefs, pushing them down my legs. Her eyes are staring at my cock like a woman starved, so I grab it and give it a couple of pumps, rubbing the precum into my skin for better lubrication going up and down. Knowing I'm not gonna be able to take her mouth, I kneel then crawl my way up her delectable body. She immediately spreads her legs as wide as she can. Since we've been together a while we've done the testing, which gives me the opportunity to go bare and feel Nora all around me when we fuck. Looking into her eyes, I lean down, and right before I place my mouth on hers, I give one jerk and I'm in deep, feeling her walls contract all around me. I have to take a minute or two to get myself under control or this is gonna end before it really gets started.

Once we both have calmed down a bit, I slowly start our dance. In and out slow, then fast, all the while I feast from her mouth, neck, and anywhere else my lips can reach. I give attention to those full perky tits of hers, with her sensitive nipples I love to nibble on. When her legs and arms tighten around me, I know she's close. I shift my hips up so every time I plunge in, I rub against her clit. Nora's soft moans are hitting my ears, making me want to take what's mine. And after a few more slow and steady strokes, I let loose and literally lose all control. My hips are moving faster than I ever thought possible, and I'm using my knees now as I drag Nora's ass onto my thighs.

Not wanting to finish before her, I know the tingles and muscle contractions are giving me the warning that I'm close. So I reach down with my finger and tap on her swollen bundle of nerves. At first, she's responsive but when I take my fingernail and press it down she flies so beautifully. Something that will stay in my mind 'til the day I die. Nora hitting her orgasm is breathtaking, but it also lets me know I can now take care of my own needs. I'm beyond anything but seeking that feeling of ecstasy. As I reach for the stars, Nora wraps me tightly, whispering dirty nothings in my ear, egging me on. When my balls pull up into my body and the butterflies in my gut are fluttering all over, the almost pain in my lower back hits right before I notice myself tense up as I feel everything releasing into Nora. My eyes close tightly as my teeth bite down on my upper lip. Feeling her slightly textured tongue licking my lips, I open and she takes control of the kiss.

When I'm done, I'm so exhausted I can barely roll my weight off of Nora, though taking her with me so our bodies keep some physical contact. Going to need at least five minutes before I can get up and make my way to the bathroom.

"My God, gorgeous, you tryin' to give me a heart attack? I literally feel like I had an out-of-body experience."

Hearing her giggle has my heart contracting. What this woman does to me.

"Bae, you good with waiting five minutes before I clean you up? And don't even say you can do it, don't want to spank that fine as fuck ass of yours, but the thought of it all pink with my handprints on it has my dick getting hard. Which is a miracle after the load I just dropped."

"I'm good, Boo, take as long as you want. If there's a wet spot you can sleep on it."

Reaching for my boxer briefs, I one-armed lift her ass up and put the boxers under her.

"See, problem solved, no wet spot. Come closer, Bae, want those lips."

Nora lifts her head, offering up her lips. I place a soft kiss on them, then holding her close we slowly drift back to sleep, arms around each other, hanging on tightly.

THREE
'GLORY'
NORA

Waking up in the same position Boo pulled me into last night, I let out a sigh. He's been putting more pressure on me about us coming out, and deep down I know he's right, but I'm so fucking scared. I don't think I'd be able to live if something ever happened to him. And since the lunatic and his bunch of assholes are still out there, there's no guarantee I can protect those closest to me.

Picking my head up, I stare at his face. My God, he's gorgeous, probably could be a model though he'd never do that, no matter how much money. He looks peaceful and so much younger than my thirty-seven-ish. Goddamn, I'm pushing thirty-eight, never thought I'd make thirty. Now I'm still here and a VP for a motorcycle club. Who would have thought that even possible? Not me.

Thought I had my life figured out. Being from a large Italian family, who figured they would have a say-so or even try to plan out how my life would go. NOT.

Obviously, they don't know Nora Winfield. *Well, duh, that's not my real name*, I think to myself. I went so to the right and vanilla when choosing my name. My only hope is that he can't find me.

I remember that last time at my townhouse in New Jersey. The 'family' wasn't happy with some of my life choices, but my parents didn't care as long as I was happy. Which is outright crazy for Italian parents, who are known for being bossy and getting their own way. I went to school and first got my BSW or Bachelor of Social Work in less than the four-year program. Yeah, I'm one of the smart kids everyone hated in school. When I graduated, told my dad I wanted to end up getting my MSW or Master of Social Work because then I could become a LSW or licensed social worker.

My dream has always been to be able to work with and, more importantly, help children. Especially ones who have been abused or mistreated in their family unit. The reasoning is pretty simple. I know I'm blessed with the family I was born into. Strict as can be but loving also. Everything my parents did for us kids was because they loved us. And at an early age, I saw what not having great parents means.

Mom has a huge heart and works as a nurse. One time she brought her work home and we all thought dad would lose his mind. But when he saw the six-year-old little boy with cigarette burns all over his body and his one little hand broken because his drug addict mother caught him stealing a piece of bread because he was starving, that did it. Dom is now part of our family since his parents unexpectedly died in a house explosion. They think it had something to do with a leaky connection and smoking dope.

When Mom brought Dom home that night, my dad called me into his office. Now I'd had an idea of what I wanted to do all my life after watching an episode of *Law & Order: Special Victims Unit*. My dream was to become the next 'Olivia Benson.' I was a teenager and she rocked being badass. So that night in my father's office, he told me that no matter what it took I was going to school and he wanted me to save as many children as I could. Having his support meant everything because to this day he supports me. Dad knows what the Devil's Handmaidens' mission is and he loves it and supports us as much as he can, though he can't tell the 'family.'

Not sure why I'm so afraid to tell Boo the main reason I'm on the run. If I want to keep him in my life, he has to know the truth and what can happen if he stays with me. Fuck, why can't it just fade away? I let it go, not that I wanted to but at the time, I had no choice. That jagoff figured a way to screw the system. Wish I had the knowledge and skills back then that I do now. Would have finished him off myself with my bare hands.

Running my hands over my face and through my hair, I can feel the tension building. Thank God, when I transferred to this chapter, I sat down with Tink, Tank, Shadow, Momma Diane, and Enforcer. Told them an abbreviated version to make sure it was okay that I stayed and became a part of this Devil's Handmaidens chapter. So if my past is about to force itself into my present, those in power already have an idea of what could show up and can somewhat prepare. So I owe that to my Boo.

Getting up is hard as shit with him wrapped all around me. Thank God I don't have an urgent need to pee. I walk to the bathroom and drop my panties that, thank God, he didn't rip last night. Then I turn on the shower and step in, pressing the steam button. I need the additional heat to penetrate my body and relax it. Boo worked me pretty good last night so a steam shower might help.

I'm so deep in my head, I don't hear the glass door open but can feel the cooler air as the steam leaves the shower. Opening my eyes, he's standing there in all his glory with a sexy as hell smirk on his face. Damn, I can't wait any longer, got to talk to him and fill in the blanks. In fact, I have to also inform my club of what's been going on with me. Didn't want to add to the mix with all the shit Vixen went through recently. And since after her drama we worked three human trafficking takedowns, I prayed my shit would go away. It didn't, so time to spill.

"Boo, morning. We can share our shower together but then I need to talk to you. Seriously, I've been putting it off for too long. And from the look on your face, don't go jumping to conclusions. I know that you're the one who doesn't care about the age difference, unlike me. For fuck's sake, what is it? I'm thirty-seven and your what again? Thirty going on thirty-one. It's only six-ish years. Why do I care what anyone else thinks? It's not a big deal so I'm going to try and let it go. And I'm not kicking you to the curb, so get that outta your melon."

"Good morning, beautiful. Feeling spunky this morning, guess my spanking wasn't enough. Might need to bring a paddle with me next time. I can see my handprints are already gone. Sure, we can talk, Nora, you know I'm always here for you, but first let's put that mouth of yours to a better use. On your knees, Bae, and open wide."

My body starts trembling as I'm not sure why I follow his orders and open wide, knowing this will take my mind off of all the other shit in there. Boo makes sure all my concentration is on the here and now, no matter what it is I'm doing. He's like velvet but hard like steel. Letting my mind go blank, I take what he gives me until I feel him pulsing in my mouth. He taps my shoulder so if I want to move back, together we'll finish him off, but today I don't want that. Need to have him lose control for once. I press into his ass cheeks and suck hard. He literally lifts onto his tippy-toes, so I reach one hand closer to the front and grab his balls, one at a time. That does it and he loses his control and rhythm. I keep mine though, and when the end comes, I'm not sure who enjoys it more. My Boo or me.

When I'm able, he lifts me off the tiled floor and helps me sit on the bench. He turns the temperature back up for the steam and first he washes off, then when I can stand, I join him and he washes me off too. When we're done, he grabs the first towel and wraps my hair up in it, then covers me with a huge bath towel. I go to the sink, pull my toothbrush out, and brush my teeth as Boo does the exact thing, though he's butt-ass naked. Not wanting to drool, I pay attention and finish my task.

Before I can place my toothbrush back in its cup, he's there giving me one of his sexy good morning kisses, which has me tingling. Those deep sapphire eyes of his are watching me, which adds to the feelings pulsing through my body. It's his deep, raspy, rough voice though that does it to me every time.

"Morning, Bae. Where you want to talk, in bed or at the table?"

Now that the time is near, I start to panic, but this conversation needs to be had today. I've followed my gut feelings since I was a teenager, so gonna follow it today. Grabbing his hand, I pull him back into bed, both our backs up against the headboard, though I'm leaning into him. Taking a deep breath and letting it out, I give Boo my story.

FOUR
'RAVEN'
BRENNA

Sitting at my desk, keeping my eyes on the four screens in front of me and the six others on my two side desks, my mind keeps running in circles. Why the fuck is Glory being so goddamn secretive? Honestly, no one cares who she lets into her bed. The problem is the sneaky shady shit on top of the bullshit of hiding who she's spending her nights with. Kind of reminds me of Shadow with Panther. What is wrong with these women? If I had a man and, shit, a hot one to boot, in my bed besides howling every night he was with me in said bed, pleasuring me, I'd be showing him off to everyone and anyone. With Glory, I'm guessing her guy's looks are off the charts ripped but not overly done. A kind of quiet guy, who'd rather listen than just talk bullshit. And just one look at him you know he can get stuff done when necessary. *Someone like Avalanche, maybe*, I wonder. No, not her type, I don't think, though they've flirted more lately. Well, since all the shit went down with Vixen in Mesquite.

My mind goes back to when I grew up. I had some really good men to compare my crushes to and they never measured up. My God, between my dad's and brothers' looks, women have always swooned over them. I don't know how my mom put up with all those women flirting with my dad, though when she brought it up, he acted like he never noticed. Then there's my brother, Ollie, who got all the best genes in our family and I'm his sister. I know a few of my club sisters have had huge crushes on him, but he only has eyes for his woman, Paisley, now. I want what my parents and brother have.

If and or when I find my soul mate, I already know I'm going to be a jealous bitch. Kinda like Shadow is with Panther. I heard how she claimed him in Mesquite when Poodles asked who he belonged to. Goddamn, wish I was there, would have given her so much shit. Badass enforcer of the Devil's Handmaidens throwing down sass over a man. Mira, as we all know her as Vixen, and the women rescued are the only ones who still call her Poodles. She's lucky Shadow knew her or the ending of that confrontation would have turned out differently for sure. I've watched our enforcer when she's doing 'wet work' and, shit, I don't know how I didn't lose my lunch for sure.

Back to Glory, it's bugging me to no end. Want to know why it's so important to keep it a secret. I mean, she's wearing pretty lacy nighties, for Christ's sake.

Those ain't for sleeping in. Trying to run through the available men handy, it's not as easy as it seems. We've got men in town we do business with or Glory would have contact with. Our trucking company and the Wooden Spirits Bar and Grill. Then there's Tank's club of brothers. Can't think of no one off hand. Finally, Ollie's bunch of ex-military. I'm racking my brain, trying to figure it out so I don't hear the door opening, but when a hand lands on my shoulder and squeezes that one touchy nerve has me almost fall off the chair onto my ass.

Turning, I can't grin because Shadow is doing everything not to bust a gut laughing. I mean, she's got red creeping up her neck to her face from what I can see with that damn tattoo of hers. And her body is shaking from holding it in. So figuring I'd help, I give her a smack on her shoulder which works. She busts out laughing like crazy.

"What do you find so frigging funny, Shadow? I could have fallen and broken something, you jackass. Now what do you want?"

"Oh, so it's not funny when someone gets you, uh, sister? You should have seen your face…. Priceless. Give me a minute, my body is trying to catch up with my mind."

Watching her laugh without a care or worry in the world is priceless. I'd never tell her that, but it's true. I've worried about this sister since I got patched in. I can see at the moment she's doing just fine. Then it dawns on me.

"You biotch, did you just get yourself some? Wait a minute, you did, didn't you? That's pure evil, Shadow, coming in here all relaxed and probably still tingly. Especially since who your man is. I bet Panther takes his time, never missing a spot, until you're a wet noodle. Ha, no pun intended."

If only I could reach for my phone and take a picture of her face right at this moment. Can't tell if she's shocked, pissed, or ready to rip my head off. Gotta let her off the hook.

"Shadow, I'm pulling your leg for scaring the shit out of me. Now, again, what can I do for you on this fine sunny day?"

She plops down in one of the two recliners against the wall and pushes the side lever that kicks the bottom up. Shit, Shadow's stretching out her legs, getting comfortable, and settling in. Great, there goes my chance to try and figure out who Glory is fucking around with.

"Raven, aren't you curious on what's going on with Glory? Just the other morning, when I got here, she was in the kitchen waiting on her coffee, dancing and shaking her ass around like crazy. And when I called her out on it, she told me to 'chill, Shadow' then giggled. Our VP giggled. Jesus Christ, what is happening to our club sister? Fuck, our club is becoming a bunch of silly in love women."

I bust a gut. Shadow obviously didn't catch what she said and by how serious she's looking; I know it's bothering her. Well, that and something else. I'm good at reading people.

"Shadow, what's really got you here in my office when you should either be in your room or at Panther's ranch relaxing after the Mesquite shitshow. Remember, I've always told you two ears and shoulders, no waiting. So if you need to get something off your chest, look, no one in line and no waiting. Spill now."

Shaking her head, I know this doesn't have anything to do with her. Even though she loves all our club sisters, there are two she's got a real soft spot for. Our prez, Tink, and Squirt.

"Thanks, sister, I'm just really worried about Goldilocks, well, ya know our prez. She's going through some shit I can't fix and it not only worries me, it pisses me off. I'm looking to let that shit out. Might just go down to the gym, try and get rid of all the anxious energy.

I watch her turn and walk right out of my room, closing the door. Well, Shadow might want to ignore shit, but that's not how I roll. Eyeballing my screens, not seeing anything out of the ordinary, I walk to the door, open it, and walk down the hallway and stop in front of Glory's door. I lean in, trying to see if I hear anything or anyone but, damn, Tink had to put in real wood doors, can't hear a damn thing.

For a split second I think about knocking but they say catching people by surprise is sometimes a good thing. My hand goes to the doorknob, I twist it, and push the door open. And lying across the bed on his stomach in nothing but boxer briefs is a perfect Adonis.

My God, damn he looks like he's carved from stone. No wonder Glory's been keeping him to herself.

Either I made a sound or moved and that somehow got his attention, because I watch that hot as hell body flex as he shifts and starts to turn on the bed, just as the bathroom door opens.

"Boo, I'm starving. You made me do all the work. Maybe I'll sneak down and get us some food. What do you…Raven, what the fuck are you doing standing there in my room? Jesus Christ, get in here and shut the door. Boo, don't turn around. Explain now, sister."

"Sister, explain yourself now. This is utter bullshit and I'm truly pissed off at you. It's one thing to hound me like a dog with a bone, but to just crash in, that just ain't right. Why do you care what or who I do? I'm a grown-ass woman, so back the hell off. Now go before I do something I might regret."

Just as I start to turn, I see a side view of who's on the bed. No way, you've got to be kidding me.

"Holy fuck, no way. You mean to tell me you're fucking *oomph*. What the hell Glory? Get off me. Damn, I don't know where that hand has been, especially seeing lover boy over there."

"Raven, seriously, if you open that big mouth of yours, you'll be sorry. Quit smirking, you little troublemaker. I'm not joking, Brenna, now get your ass out of my room and again, keep your mouth shut. We're both adults, it's none of your business. Get.

I open the door and walk out with it hitting my backside from the force Glory slammed the door. I head downstairs to the kitchen because I need a coffee fix and the little one in my room won't do it. Need one of those fancy coffees from that huge fucking machine Tink bought not too long ago. I'm smiling to myself and literally plow right into Noodles, who puts his hands on my arms to stop me from falling back.

"Oh, shit, sorry, Noodles, didn't see you. Had my mind on other stuff. Why you up, everything okay?"

"Yeah, we're good, Raven, thanks for asking. Sweet Pea wanted some ginger ale so came down to get it for her. Everything good with you?"

As we shoot the shit for a few minutes, I know what I found out tonight is either going to help me or make my life a living hell. Only time will tell because I now know who Glory's Boo is. And damn…can't believe it for a second.

FIVE
'GLORY'
NORA

"Goddamn it. It's gonna come out now about you and me, Boo, and it won't be pretty. That sister, she's got a mouth the size of a hippo, for Christ's sake. She can't keep a secret, even if someone promised her a million dollars. Damn, we don't need this right now. The club is finally starting to settle down. After Vixen's drama, including her announcement of her pregnancy, life has started to calm down. This could, son of a bitch, with our club still involved with that racist group and trying to break up their circuit, don't need any more drama. Boo, you got nothing to say? Aren't you upset?"

He just stares at me with those beautiful eyes, saying nothing. He flips over and then sits up. In a second, he's on his feet picking his jeans off the floor, then his shirt, before sitting and grabbing his socks and boots. I just stand here watching him get dressed. What is wrong with him? We need to talk about this and he's just gonna up and run. Great, when the going gets tough my Boo just leaves. I go to grab his arm and he steps back so I can't.

"Do me a favor, Nora, don't touch me. Forget about this shit we been doing, seems like it's something ya already regret, so I'm gonna go back home and you can get on with whatever you need to. I'll see ya around."

No fucking way am I letting him walk out on me. Not after all we've shared. I'm not doing this right so this time I grab his arm, pulling on it as he walks by. I didn't even see it coming, but one minute I have my hand gripping his upper arm and the next I'm in a squat all wrapped up with him on top of me, his legs securing mine down while his hands are wrapped around my upper arms, holding me down.

"I told you not to touch me, Bae. Now I'm gonna go. If we bump into each other, might be better if we keep it personable but distant. Again, sorry this shit was, fuck, I don't even know. Thought you were different, Nora, but guess not. Another crazy female who can't see what's right in front of her own nose."

In less than five seconds he is off me and walking out the door, though he stops when he steps into the hallway, turns around, and literally pulls my heart out of my chest.

"We had something, or at least I thought we were working toward it. Then you go and act like a high school girl who doesn't want her friends to know she's dating. Well, sorry to inform you, *Glory*, but one day I hope you look back and see what you gave up, and the funny thing is, I have no idea why you're so afraid to let others know you're involved with me. I'm a grown-ass man who served our country, and now I'm a brother with the Intruders so not a fuckin' bum. Makes me feel like shit, gotta tell ya."

With his eyes on me, I walk toward him and know he won't hurt me, even if his life depended on it. I reach out with both hands and grab his arms, pulling him back into my room. Once he's back in my room and the door is closed, I wrap my arms around his neck and stand really close to him. His arms stay rigid at his sides, telling me how pissed off he is. Then I give it to him, no holding back.

"Boo, before coming out to Montana and joining the Devil's Handmaidens, well shit, before I was involved in the Handmaidens club out East, something happened that really fucked with me. I met Gino in first year of college and, long story short, I got pregnant and we got married. We had Lilly and our lives were on the road to awesome. Then his brother, Oscar, started getting weirder and weirder. Things started happening that we couldn't explain. Then I got pregnant again and we were beyond excited. When I was maybe eight or ten weeks pregnant our home was broken into. It was Gino's brother, Oscar, and our nightmare began. He held me captive as his prisoner for over two years. For the first two weeks he beat me daily until I lost my baby. Then the sadist in him came out.

"Not sure how, but since the Devil's Handmaidens mission out East is very similar to ours here in Montana, which is to save trafficked and abused women and children. When Harlow, Peppermint, and Momma somehow heard some gossip about a crazy as fuck dude holding women against their will and pimping them out, they took action. That's what happened, they broke down the door and saw me chained to the wall. They rescued me along with two other girls, also chained to walls in the other bedrooms. He was also abusing and pimping them out. Momma almost killed him with hot oil and a cast iron skillet. That day changed my life forever. Even after all this time, I still have moments when I fear the day will come when he gets out and comes after me because he's been very vocal that he blames me. He threatened and yelled that I will never have anyone in my life because it was my fault the Devil's Handmaidens had him on their radar. Doesn't matter it was his huge mouth and asshole ways that brought the club looking for him because he was bragging about the whores he could do anything to, and he would pimp them out for the right amount of money. After I was a member and shit kept coming my way, my prez came to me, asking if I wanted to transfer to get away from everything, and I jumped at the chance.

"That's how I came here to Timber-Ghost and to the Devil's Handmaidens in Montana. Tink and I hit it off, though Shadow and I had to do some work. She thought I was going to take Tink away from her. Once she realized I just wanted—no, needed—some sort of family in my life she chilled out. When Tink offered me the VP patch, I jumped at it. Our old VP took off with her ol' man, who was going up to Alaska to work the pipeline.

He was some kind of an engineer. She's kept in touch with the sisters over the years. And to this day I've never heard from Gino. Raven has tried to find him and Lilly, but it's like they disappeared from the face of the earth.

"So yeah, I'm scared shitless to share about us to anyone because you're special to me, and I don't want to take a chance that the lunatic or whoever he's associated with would get wind. If something happened to you, don't know what I'd do. Please don't leave me."

Watching his face, I see it when he gets why I am like I am. Grabbing me close, he draws me in and holds on tightly. I can't lose him too. I don't care who finds out, as long as he's with me I can handle anything.

SIX
'TINK'
MAGGIE\GOLDILOCKS

I'm sitting at the old desk Pops gave me when Shadow and I started the Devil's Handmaidens club, back in the day, in our clubhouse in town. What I'm about to do goes against everything that is me but I'm worried as shit about my VP and friend. For months I've noticed Glory isn't herself, and watching her with Olivia is the only time she seems even relatively happy. That little girl, even with everything she's been through, is coming out of her shell nicely.

And to my utter surprise, all she can talk about is when she's old enough she's going to become a Devil's Handmaidens sister. One of the sisters, not sure who, maybe Peanut or Heartbreaker came into town and had our seamstress at the cleaners make a mini kutte for Olivia. The look on that little girl's face was priceless. She ran right to Glory to show her favorite person in the world how she's an 'honorary' mini sister of the club.

My VP watched her with such love and adoration in her eyes it was awesome to see.

Besides that, Glory has become half of the person she used to be. Not sure why as we have no pending cases that we are working on currently, except the continued one trying to break up the Thunder Cloud Knuckle Brotherhood. Though that shouldn't be any concern to Glory the only connection is our club as far, as I know.

So deep in thought I literally jump at the double knock on the door, which tells me it's my VP.

"Come on in, Glory."

The door opens and she walks in. Damn, she looks tired for sure but there is something else in her eyes I can't make out. Maybe despair, worry, or shit, she looks scared. What the hell is going on?

"Hey, Tink, you texted you wanted to see me? Something going on or did we get another trafficking circuit we need to bring down and break up? Shit, we still have some of the women and children from Juice's. I know some of the women went back to their families but the others are still here on the ranch. I know for a fact two of them want to stay permanently and are working to learn ranch duties with some of the sisters. From what I hear, one is really good with the large animals, while the other is pretty handy with a hammer. She's been helping check fencing and shit like that."

"Yeah, I heard the same thing. Thank God we were able to place those babies with either their mommas or in that protective group Ironside knew. That was a whole lot of work taking care of all those little ones.

Though not why I called you here, Glory. We need to talk and I need you to be honest. Need to know what's going on with you because, sister, you aren't yourself."

Head hanging down, her hair shifts forward, hiding her face. She leans forward putting her elbows on my desk, hands on her forehead. I can feel the tension and something else coming off of her in waves. Shit, I don't want to lose her as my VP, but especially as my friend. I know enough about her backstory but never really pried into her past.

"Tink, fuck me, I thought this would settle but it's not. To start, I didn't intentionally not tell you, but life happened and for once I'm on the road to finding my happy. And I'm stalling. So, I'm kind of seeing someone. You know him but give me a minute or two to keep it to myself before I share. The reason is complicated. Do you remember what happened when I was back with the Devil's Handmaidens MC in the Atlantic City, New Jersey chapter? Not sure if Harlow ever told you, but they rescued me from a horrific situation. Fuck, just to talk about it has my skin crawling. I married my high school sweetheart during my first year of college. Yeah, I was also pregnant. As an Italian Catholic girl with child, my father and brothers didn't really give Gino a chance, though he already told me we were getting married when I told him I was pregnant. That was always our dream, finish school, get married, and have lots of babies. We had Lilly, who was a perfect baby from the start. With the help of my folks, we bought a fixer-upper and started our lives together. Gino's family is in construction, so needless to say they were involved in the fixing up, especially his brother, Oscar. Whenever he was around, I was uncomfortable because he gave me the willies. Not to mention he was fixated on our daughter, Lilly.

"One day I had gone to the grocery store, had Lilly with me. I forgot something at the beginning of the aisle and went to get it. When I turned, my cart and Lilly were gone. I lost myself screaming, yelling, and running up and down the aisles. When I finally got to the freezer area, my cart was there with Lilly in the front, and Oscar was standing off to the side watching her. When I called his name, he turned and with a crazy look in his eyes, told me, "Better watch this princess, 'cause next time you might not find her." Then he turned and walked away.

"After that I became frantic, never wanting to leave Lilly alone. As she got older Gino and I found out I was pregnant again. This time though I was sick day and night. Gino was so worried he told his dad he wanted to work close to home if at all possible. His dad was and is awesome, so he said yes. Oscar got jealous, bitching constantly that Gino wasn't pulling his weight in the family business. No one knew what his problem was but he was known to go off the deep end from time to time, according to Gino.

"One night we were in bed when we heard someone kick in our door downstairs. Gino ran to the wall safe, pulling out two Glocks and clips. He handed one to me and kept one for himself. Lilly was sleeping right next door so I motioned that I was going through our walk-in closet to the cheat door to her room.

"I wasn't in her room for even a minute or two when I heard Gino screaming and swearing. Then a single shot sounded and it was suddenly dead quiet. I lifted Lilly out of her little big girl bed and walked back into the closet, locking the little door. I reached down, pulled the carpet back, and placed Lilly in the secret safe room Gino insisted on when he was working on the closet. His family had some distant ties to some, as my husband said 'criminals' and he wasn't taking any chances with his girls. I just finished putting the rug down and pulling the suitcase over it when I heard a noise behind me. Turning, I saw Oscar with a weird as fuck look on his face. Then he turned my heart to stone and my life to hell.

"Bitch, get over here now. You're done teasing me. I'm taking what should have been mine from the get-go. I was the first one to ask you out but you said, *"No sorry, Oscar, not looking to date right now."* I believed you and thought I'd give you some time. Then what do you do? Gino asks you out and you jump at it. What the fuck? I wasn't good enough, for Christ's sake. Then you fucked him and had Lilly. Now you're knocked up again. Your pussy is gonna be like an airport runway, but goddamn I've waited enough.'

"Seeing the Glock on the shelf where I put it, I lunged for it. Oscar realized what I was gonna do and moved like a cheetah. When I reached for it, he grabbed my arm, twisting it around my back, pulling me against him. When I felt his hardness against me, I froze. No, this can't be happening, he's my brother-in-law. Where is Gino, why isn't he helping me? It was like this maniac was in my head because he answered my question.

"Your husband is on the front room floor bleeding out. So either you come with me quietly, or I'll go back down and rape his ass before I slit his throat while you watch, then I'll grab you and we'll be gone. Either way you, my little whore, are coming with me. Make up your mind now. Wait a minute, where the fuck is my lil' princess Lilly?"

"I knew, Tink, that he would either kill her or worse, ruin her life. I did the only thing I could. I lied through my teeth.

"Oscar, she's with my parents. Mom wanted to take her to work tomorrow as I guess it's grandparents' day or some crap like that. Please, can we talk about this? You're Gino's brother and family. I didn't mean to hurt your feelings back then but, Oscar, we have a family, Gino and me. Don't do this, your father will kill you. You know that."

"Just mentioning his father, he ground his dick into my ass then let my arm go, swinging me around to face him. His face was filled with hate and something else. True madness.

"Bitch, what did I tell you? You're mine now, and when I'm done, I'll sell your ass and make a little money. Then I'll grab that little brat you and my brother bred together. I like them young, though she'd be my first little girl. I'll train her so when the time comes, she'll be ready. Now let's go. Move your ass woman no games, I mean it."

"Walking in front of him, I carefully moved down the stairs to the front door.

"Baby! My God, Oscar, what are you doing with my wife? For Christ's sake, don't do this, Brother. We can work this out. Come on."

"Oscar stopped and looked at his brother on the floor, bleeding from—God, I don't even know—he's covered in blood. His face is pale and he's starting to tremble.

"Gino, I'm gonna give you a choice. Either you let me take this bitch and I let you live. Or I'll still take her anyway after I cap your ass and go to this bitch's momma's house tomorrow and grab your brat. Those are your options so pick, Brother."

"I watched Gino whose face was filled with so much pain. I knew before he said it what his decision was. I would do the same if I was in his position.

"Oscar, leave Lilly alone. I've had my fill of this whore, so go ahead take her. Just know I'm not gonna lie when everyone wants to know what happened. You hear me, Brother, Mom and Dad will know it was you."

"No, dear brother, they won't. They're getting cold on their kitchen floor. So might want to rethink your threat. You'll tell everyone this cheating bitch was hittin' it with some banger and that's whose baby she's carrying. Make sure everyone knows she walked out on you and the brat. Now give your wife a goodbye 'cause you'll never see her again, that's a promise. But you will see me again, dear brother, guarantee. You now work for me."

"Gino looked at me with so much pain in his eyes but didn't say a single word. When he nodded so did I.

The life we knew would never be ours ever again. Oscar grabbed me and walked me out to a van. He threw me in the back, handcuffing me to a bar on the wall of the rusty vehicle. I'm sure you can put two and two together on what happened next. I never even had a clue how obsessed he was with me. Oscar hid it well. I was held captive for two years, four months, seven days, and thirteen hours. One day Oscar got lax as I was cooking dinner. The door busted open and there was Harlow, Peppermint, and Mama. They took one look at the thick cuff on my ankle that was attached to a chain bolted into the concrete wall. I was never left loose. Mama saw that snake of a chain and everything it stood for. She walked up to me, putting her hand on my cheek then grabbed the hot skillet, turned, and threw it at Oscar. He screamed like a little bitch so Mama swung, hitting him on his shoulder. He went down immediately. The rest is, like they say, history.

"Well, I've done some reaching out and according to Harlow that jagoff motherfucker is still in jail. He threatened me that I would never have anyone in my life or between my legs because he owned me. Since I've become part of the Timber-Ghost chapter, I've not had any weird shit happen. Since I've gotten together with my Boo, late night calls and hang-ups started, strange stuff shows up on my cage, and stuff is left by my bike in public lots when I park. Now, could be anyone, but I'm afraid somehow Oscar found out and is making sure the threat he's made to me is still, what can I say, real. I'm worried this will spread to my sisters and maybe even Olivia. Don't know what to do, Prez. I care deeply for each and every Devil's Handmaidens sister in our club. Not to mention all the families. I love what I do, but if it comes down to it I could leave, maybe relocate, just to make sure no one is hurt by my past baggage because Oscar is a psychopathic maniac. If he can, he will ruin anyone around me. I can't have him put his filthy eyes on any of you or Olivia."

I look at my right hand, my VP, realizing that's the most she's given me about her past ever, which tells me she's worried and worse, scared. Son of a bitch, we can't catch a break between all the sisters' drama. Though this has multiple situations that need to be addressed. So going to dive in.

"Your *Boo*, Glory. Come on, you think I don't know? No, don't go there, I'll respect your wish for now, but don't think I've not had my finger on this since it started. Don't ask because only one other knows and that's because she figured it out before me."

"Yeah, Raven found out and I'm afraid she's going to run her mouth off to everyone."

"No, not talking about our nerdy girl, Raven, but the other pain in my ass and yours."

It takes her a minute, but when it hits Glory, I see it and burst out laughing. Her face gives it away. She's got to be thinking that out of every one of our sisters, why that one? Glory is so fucked.

"Since you figured out who it is, she's waiting for me to let her know she can come in. Is that okay with you, Glory?"

She nods as I reach down and type in a quick text. We sit and it doesn't take but minutes and there's a knock on the door.

"Come on in, my own pain in the ass."

The door is flung open and there stands Zoey, a huge smile on her face. I feel so bad for Glory, but she had to have known that secrets never stay that way in this club. I watch my bestie walk in, closing the door, then taking a seat next to my VP. They have a stare off, which to my surprise my bestie shifts her eyes first. But her sharp tongue has not lost any of the fierceness.

"Goldilocks, you owe me that hundred dollars 'cause I was right and you were wrong. Told you it was a dick that had her head all fucked up. Now, come on, tell us who he is, Glory. All I pray is that it isn't Big Bird. That, sister, would cause me to lose my motherfucking mind. Just sayin' though, I want you to be happy and to get yourself some so I'll try not to go off the deep end too bad. I could see why you'd be attracted to the man, he's one fine piece of bird feathers. Don't tell Panther I said that, please."

I can't help it; I break out laughing at my bestie's attempt to try and put Glory at ease. And from the huge smile on our VP's face, Zoey is doing a great job. Until Glory replies right back at her.

"Thank God you'll be able to live with it, Shadow, because we got married last week and I'm having his baby."

Zoey's mouth drops open and her eyes bug out, which is scary as hell with that freaking skull tattoo on her face. Glory gives me a wink and, fuck me, I can't believe she got one over on our club enforcer. Zoey won't ever be able to live this one down if Glory decides to tell all the Devil's Handmaidens sisters. I can tell my bestie is confused as hell and not sure what to do or say. So I decide to help her out.

"Come on, Glory, tell Shadow you're joking before we have to call either Dr. Cora to help with the shock you've put her into, or put a call out to Panther so he can pull her back from the ledge."

Glory actually lets a loud chuckle out then looks at Zoey.

"Shadow, calm your ass. No, I'm not pregnant or worse, married to Avalanche. And I never understood why you call him Big Bird, but now isn't the time to ask. Who I'm involved with isn't my biggest issue, though it's weighing on my mind. One, because he's younger than me—not by much—but still I'm sure some will have shit to say. Second, he has ties to some who are very close to our club and not sure how that will be received. And three, I'm getting some calls and hang-ups that have me concerned. Guess now is the time to explain why I left the Atlantic City Chapter.

"As you both know I was an abused and tortured woman before I hooked my star to Harlow and Peppermint after they rescued me. I had a really rough time trying to acclimate into regular life and they helped me. They not only rescued me but gave me a home until I was able to try and restart my life. The Devil's Handmaidens Atlantic City Chapter literally saved me and then gave me a chance to find my path in life. I felt like I owed them and had nothing else in my life. Oscar was in jail, but he had hung around with a white supremacy group. They were growing and had some huge influences within their group and the country. Knowing the Devil's Handmaidens club's mission was to rescue trafficked victims, and even though I wasn't trafficked per se, I was being abused, beaten, and prostituted out. I was speaking to Harlow on what my choices in life were and she offered to sponsor me if I wanted to throw my hand in to prospect. The rest I believe you both know. When the offer came to move out to Timber-Ghost, Montana, I looked at it as a fresh start. I had no idea where my husband, Gino, and Lilly went. And I lost the baby from all the beatings and physical abuse from Oscar in the beginning of my time in his hell, which I think was his plan all along. Only thing God did right was I never got pregnant from Oscar. And believe me that prick tried.

"Now I'm with a new man and Olivia is in my life and I'm worried like crazy. I can't be responsible if something was to happen to either of them. And I'm not forgetting all of my sisters in the club. It's been weighing on me, and maybe the only solution is for me to pack up and move on. Not sure where I'd go, and believe me don't want to leave, but I just might have to if my back is against the wall."

"ARE YOU FUCKING NUTS, NORA?? There is no way we are letting you run away because you're afraid. NO, don't, enough of you talking, now you're gonna listen, sister. Goldilocks, me, and all the other sisters are here for you, but you need to let us in. Quit holding everyone at arm's length. Knock that shit off now. There is nothing we can't handle together. And you know why…because we're fucking family. So what's gotten under your skin so deep that you, of all sisters, think running is the answer? And who's this spineless dick who would let you even consider hitting the road and leaving the home you found for yourself? Must be a real prick, your younger piece of meat."

All three of us literally jump out of our chairs when a throat clears from where the door is wide open. I look that way and can feel the shock run through my body as I see who's there and how he's looking at my VP. Holy shit, Glory's guy is him? No fucking way. Then he opens his mouth.

"Shadow, I'm not a prick or spineless. I can't make Nora do anything she doesn't want to. What I do try to do is support her in whatever her decisions are and hope they include me. Not sure why you think she's getting ready to hit the road, as she's the one who told me to meet you three here. Bae, guess this is you taking that first step, right? Would have been nice if you had shared with me your plans so I maybe could have been prepared and not thrown me to these sisters of Satan, no pun intended."

Watching the two of them I see what neither of them are acknowledging. They are totally and madly in love. One thing stands out to me, so being nosy, I have to ask.

"What does Bae stand for?"

He looks at me for a brief second before his eyes search out Glory's. The moment stands still and even my bestie for once keeps her mouth shut. Then he shocks the shit out of me while never taking his eyes from Glory.

"Bae means 'before anyone else.' And that is what Nora means to me, she comes before anyone else."

I hear Zoey take in a deep breath as her head drops. Knowing her as I do, she's trying to hide how much what he just said touched her, the big softie that she is. Glory gets up and walks to him, putting her hands at his waist, dropping her head onto his chest.

All I can think is *damn, they look phenomenal together.* That's my thought right before I see walking through the door there is Noodles, Panther, and Avalanche. When Avalanche sees Glory and her guy together, he looks confused for a minute or two before he starts cracking up like the lunatic he is.

"No fucking way. When Panther told me that skull anii' was meeting here to figure out who Glory was banging, I had to come and see. Well, fuck me, guess I jerked around too long. My man, good for you, you stealthy sneaking bastard. And you, woman, shit, Glory, you'll never know what you missed out on. I got moves no other man has, just sayin'."

He's gyrating his hips like crazy. Those moves and what he just said has everyone in my office starting to snicker and laugh. Zoey is holding her gut, mouth open like she's ready to puke. As usual, leave it to Avalanche and his magical personality to be able to break up the tension in the room. Damn, wish I could figure out one of my single sisters who would be a good match for him. He deserves only the best, as he's been through enough hell from what Zoey has shared with me.

My eyes move to Glory, who's held tightly by her man and my father's favorite prospect, Yoggie. Damn, my dad is gonna lose his mind as I'm sure he probably has no idea. Shit's going to fly, thank God Mom will be able to calm his ass down, eventually. Again a Devil's Handmaidens sister hooks her star to an Intruder brother or soon-to-be brother. I can't keep up with these women.

Feeling eyes, I look to see Noodles watching me closely. I give him a huge smile, which he returns with an eyebrow lifted up. I shrug my shoulders which has him chuckling. He knew what he was getting into hooking his star to the president of a motorcycle club. All I can hope is that Glory doesn't have the drama we all had when we found our men.

SEVEN
'YOGGIE'
SEBASTIAN

Watching this group of people, I know they only want the best for my Bae. I'm worried about her if these phone calls keep coming. No one says a word when she picks it up, they just breathe hard so Nora can hear it. I think the hang-ups are worse because the person waits to hear her voice then waits a few seconds before they hang up.

I know Nora is worried about Olivia, but I think that little girl is in the safest place she could be now that she's away from Juice. Between the Devil's Handmaidens MC and my club, the Intruders, we'll all keep our eyes on that little girl. And personally, I won't let anyone near Olivia. They'll have to get through my dead body first.

Feeling her close, I shift my attention to all that is Nora. When she's right next to me, she grabs my hand and pulls me into her. Not caring who's in the room since I've waited forever to be able to do this, I pull her up to me and hear her gasp. Holding her under the arms, I lift until she's on her tiptoes. Then I lower my head and take my first official kiss in public with my Bae. Never thought we'd get to this point....public PDA. Feeling her smile against my lips, I lift my head an inch.

"Having fun, Boo?"

"Totally, Bae. Now what?"

"You trust me, Sebastian? First we'll rip the Band-Aid off quickly. Ready?"

Then she grabs my hand, pulling me out of Tink's office and down the hall. When it finally dawns on me what she's about to do, we enter the common area of their club. Some of the sisters are lounging or playing video games, while the twins are playing pool. I watch as Nora puts her fingers between her lips into her mouth and a shrieking whistle comes out, catching everyone's attention.

"Listen up, sisters. Gonna do this once and only once. This hot, sexy, and very single man is now mine. That means we're together so make sure you lil' honey bitches find your own man. That is all."

Then she reaches up and plants a hot and heavy kiss on my lips, while in the background all I can hear are hoots, howls, and obscene sounds, until a door slams and a booming voice rocks the room.

"What the ever-lovin' fuck is goin' on? Yoggie, get your fuckin' hands off my girl now. Prospect, I won't repeat myself, so better listen and do it now. Glory girl, get your fine ass over here. Did I just walk into *The Twilight Zone*? Jesus Christ, is this the next drama in my baby girl's goddamn club? This better not turn into the next circus because not sure how much more I'm gonna be able to take. How many more of my girls are left who are single?"

No one says a word so I look around. Every single Devil's Handmaidens sister is looking at Tank like a little girl looks at her daddy who's her hero. Not sure what I'm seeing so I glance down at Nora, who's eyes are wet and locked with my president's. She lets my hand go and walks toward the big man.

"Tank, I'm sorry I didn't come to you but don't be mad at Sebastian, please. I care about him. I don't want him to get into trouble because it was me who begged him to keep this relationship a secret."

Then she gets on her toes and leans up, whispering in his ear. I watch my prez's face get serious as his eyes get bigger and bigger. When they shoot my way, I don't shy away. As much as I want to be an Intruder, I'll pull out quicker than you can blink if it's a choice between Nora and the club. It must show on my face because Tank continues to stare until he smirks and gives me a chin lift. Thank God, because besides the military I've never felt more at home than I do with the Intruders. Great bunch of men who kinda all have the same way of thinking and values like I do.

I walk over to Tank, never taking my eyes off of him. When I'm close enough for him to hear me, I try out how to put the words but just let my mouth loose.

"Prez, I know you look at the women in the Devil's Handmaidens like your daughters, so I'm gonna ask if I can continue to see Nora. And before you say yay or nay, just so you know, this is just me showing respect. She's mine and ain't no one gonna say different."

Tank smiles hugely then leans down to Nora, whispering something. She throws her head back and laughs. He joins her then they both look at me. I shrug my shoulders as I have no idea what's going on but give my girl a grin anyway.

"Son, you don't have to ask me anything. That you did shows me the type of man you are. I like that. All I got to say is if you hurt her, I'll beat the living shit outta ya then turn you over to Wrench and Enforcer. You know though, you hurt Glory and no one will be able to hold Shadow back, so keep that in the back of your mind. Out of the three of those psychos, I put my money on my girl, Shadow. Now, congratulations to both of ya. Enjoy this time as it passes way too fast. And if you both can, try for no fuckin' drama, murder, and mayhem. My daughter's club seems to attract it."

He gives Nora a quick hug and shakes my hand, then walks toward Tink's office. Looking around, I think to myself, *this went easier than I thought it would.* Feeling pretty good, I pull Nora into my side just as the door opens and kids of all ages run in. Oh fuck, Taz and Vixen are here with the children. Now the real test, as I see Olivia searching for that familiar face she knows. When she sees Nora, she smiles huge and skips toward us. When she sees my hand around Nora's waist, she slows down then stops.

"Why you got your hands on Glory?"

"Cariño, manners, please. First this is Sebastian, but his brothers call him Yoggie. He's my friend and hopefully yours too."

I watch her looking between the both of us, fear on her face. Not sure why until she mutters the most horrendous thoughts I've ever heard come from a young person's mouth.

"Glory, does that mean he'll want to touch me too? Like that man let others at that house far away? He's darker than them, but I guess a man is a man, right? Should I go in the back and take my clothes off?"

Nora sucks in a deep breath and when I look down, she's looking at Olivia with such a pained expression. I can't even think, but I move Nora slightly then walk to Olivia, hands out. She doesn't move and barely breathes. I don't even notice that the room has gone eerily quiet. Kneeling in front of the terrified girl, I put my hands in front of me. She looks at them first then at my face, searching for something, not sure what. Then hesitantly she puts those tiny hands in my huge mitts. She's giving me her trust and that is something I will never abuse.

"Little Olivia, listen closely to me. See these big hands of mine? They will never hurt you, ever. Since we are now in each other's lives, this is a promise I'll make to you. No one will ever hurt you as long as I'm here. And just so you know, I don't make promises I can't keep. Now about Nora, she means something to me and you mean something to her, so can we try and be friends?"

Olivia leans to the left to see Nora. I don't know what

she did but Olivia smiles her way. Then she moves closer to me, pulling her hands out of mine, and throwing her arms around my neck. Oh damn, this kid is gonna kill me. I put my hands around her waist and stand up. With Olivia in my arms I walk to Nora, who puts her hand on Olivia's back, rubbing up and down.

Looking around I see everyone grinning or just watching us closely. Then someone in the back starts laughing hard. People separate and there is Raven, a huge smile on her face, walking toward us.

"So, it's finally out now? Glory, you told me not to say a word, almost made me slice myself so we could do a blood handshake. I come out and see you, Yoggie Bear, and little bear all huddled together in front of the entire club. So why did ya tell me to keep it quiet? Not cool, sister, not cool. My feelings are hurt."

Olivia shifts and looks from Glory to Raven then back at Glory. Then she leans her head on my shoulder and sighs.

"Miss Raven, don't be mad. Yoggie just promised to keep me safe and won't put his big mitts on me. I'm happy he's with Glory. Did you like Yoggie and are you mad that they are together? Remember Poodles, she had a favorite saying she would tell the other girls. Something like *there are tons of fish in the sea.* Maybe you can find another fish."

Watching Raven's face is priceless. Her eyes get big when Olivia tells her I have her back and that I'll never hurt her. Now I'm not sure what she's feeling because she's trying to hold something in. Then she busts out cackling.

"Little sister, no, I don't like Yoggie Bear in that way. I'm glad Glory and Yoggie are together. And your Poodles is right there are thousands, if not millions, of fish in the sea. Maybe I need to start fishing, great idea. You want to go with me, lil' Olivia, and help me catch my own fishy?"

Olivia starts to giggle, which is cute as hell. Then she replies to Raven.

"Miss Raven, I'm too young to try and look for a fish. I got to grow up more and don't think Glory wants me to find a boyfriend yet, even though I kind of promised Teddy. Do you want me to wait, Glory?"

"Cariño, yes, I do. Maybe when you're sixteen, or wait, I think we should wait until you're thirty then we can talk again. Until then you and Teddy can be best of friends."

Nora starts giggling then starts to tickle Olivia, who is now laughing out loud. Then everyone starts to join in. I take it all in because this is a first. The whole family thing is a new experience. Foster care homes didn't have any of this ever. Looking at Tank, he gives me a chin lift and smiles at me.

EIGHT
'GLORY'
NORA

It's been just a few weeks since Sebastian and I came out and it's been wonderful. When Enforcer asked me to stop by their clubhouse one night on my way home from the Wooden Spirits Bar and Grill, I was surprised but also curious as hell. Since Olivia was again at Taz's, I didn't have anything else going on, so I told him sure.

When I finally pull off on the road that leads to the Intruders clubhouse, my mind is all over. God, please, I hope nothing happened to Sebastian, but I would think Enforcer would have said something.

What else could it be, I'm thinking as I get out of my cage and walk toward the door. I see Slick standing on the outside. I hear that Tank called him back for something which he needed Slick's help. Slick's a strange nut to break for sure. That he's still breathing after all that went down with Taz and the Devil's Handmaidens MC is surprising. Why the hell Tank and Brick wanted him breathing I'll never know. Well yeah, they did give Slick to Chains to get as much information out of him as possible about the Thunder Cloud Knuckle Brotherhood. From what I hear that crazy fucker did not go easy on Slick. And he got everything out of him. But Chains was warned not to end Slick's life, so he didn't. Though he's missing a pinky and a few toes. Also, some teeth and patches of skin.

"Evening, Glory. How ya doing tonight?"

"Hanging in, Slick, all I can do. Hear you're going back to the Grimm Wolves soon after that shit with Dingo. You all healed? Any idea what I'm about to walk into?"

"I'm not at liberty to talk about anything. Remember I'm a prospect, well lower than that, but there's no name for it. Though you heard right, leaving next week to go back home. That's what it is now, just had to help Tank out with that brotherhood bunch of assholes. Let me get this door for ya. Enjoy your night, Glory."

He opens the door and it sounds like one hell of a party. Walking through, no one notices me, but I see that everyone in here is feeling no pain. Glancing around I see Wrench, Enforcer, Pussy, and Half Pint by the bar, each with a beer in their hands. Most of the prospects are in the far corner talking and laughing. There are sweet butts all over the party room serving drinks or sitting on laps, making sure the Intruders are happy. Nothing too indecent but nonetheless, not what I want to see. Something catches my eye and I turn my head to see a half-naked bitch with her hands on Sebastian. What the ever-lovin' fuck? Before I can lose my shit further, he pushes her hands off of him, taking a step back.

I walk in that direction, hands in fists at my side. That's when everyone notices I'm in the building. The crowd actually parts to let me by as I make my way to my ol' man. The bitch actually has her hip cocked as well as a hand on it, and a very ugly look on her face. When I'm within hearing distance, she lets loose.

"What's up, Glory? Coming to share your 'cock' with me? I'm good with that, Yoggie likes threesomes, so this should be interesting. What do you want, the top or middle? I'll take whatever you don't want. I'm very flexible."

Without even thinking, I swing back then connect with her jaw. First punch. My second hit is a kick and the third lands in her midsection and I hear the air leave her lungs. My fourth and last punch lands on her nose, which instantly starts pouring blood. Then as I try to get closer, I'm lifted from behind and pulled farther back.

"Bae, don't even go there. I'm no saint but I'd never go there and risk losing you. Come on, Nora, think for a second. Whatcha doing here anyway?"

"Enforcer called me and told me to stop by on my way back to the ranch. Any idea why or is this a normal weekday party?"

Before Sebastian can say a single word, I hear a whistle I've come to know. It's Enforcer and when I turn, he's standing next to Tank. When the president of the Intruders sees me he grins, then motions me to come over to him. I grab Sebastian's hand and together we walk to where Tank is. He reaches out and gives me a quick hug. Then he reaches out and grabs Sebastian's arm, pulling him to his side.

Again Enforcer whistles, though this time longer and louder. Everyone stops what they are doing and looks in the direction the noise came from. When the entire group of men are looking at Tank, he slaps Sebastian on the back.

"All right, not big on tons of words or bullshit, so gonna get right to it. Talked it over with the brothers and everyone is on board. Yoggie, we all see your dedication, determination, and desire to be an Intruder. You will still be on a sort of probation but congratulations, brother, and welcome to your forever home. Enforcer, go call Georgie, tell him to get his ass up here to the clubhouse, need him to tattoo our newest Intruder brother. Freak, give me that bag now. Okay, you've stepped up to the plate so many times, Yoggie, that after some thought we've decided to patch your ass in now. We'll get a party scheduled for ya, but tonight you get these patches: the center club logo one and the top and bottom rockers. We'll get Momma Diane to sew them on while you and Georgie figure out what your club tat is going to be and where. Then you'll get it tonight, so plan on a long as fuck one and no booze, it thins the blood. Glory, if you can stay I'm sure our boy would appreciate the company. Now, one shot and then we got shit to do, can't hold your hand all the time, Yoggie. To our newest brother, we welcome you to be free with what you decide, to ride every day with the wind at your back and the sun on your face, and hold on to those who are important to ya. Congratulations, my brother Yoggie."

I hear congrats and hoots, hollers, and all kinds of interesting comments, including that we should get a room to celebrate and get down and dirty. Fucking assholes.

Feeling arms pulling me back, I shiver when Sebastian's entire front pressed tightly and super close. I feel every muscle, and I mean each one, especially the one pressing into my ass. Damn, this man can get my juices flowing just by being close.

"Nora, do ya mind hanging around with me while I get my tattoo? Already know what I want, but it's a good size so if you got shit to do, I understand. I had no idea that this was going to go down tonight but, Bae, I appreciate you stopping by and being a part of it."

"Sebastian, let me call Taz, see if she can keep an eye on Olivia until I get back. If not, Shadow is around and she loves hanging with my girl. Or any of the sisters, just depends who's at the ranch. And I'd love to stay and keep you company. I'm so proud of you, and just so you know, this is something you've earned and deserve. Now let me make my call, then I'm all yours."

Walking away, I already have my phone in hand, looking up Taz's home number, when someone plows into my front so hard I fall backward and land hard on my ass.

"Goddamn you, asshole. Next time open your eyes and watch where the hell you're going."

Looking up I see Malice looking down at me, giving me a disgusted look. He doesn't offer me a hand up or even apologizes. Just looks me up and down, smirks, then turns to walk away. His attitude pisses me off so much I leap to my feet, swearing under my breath. He's been an asshole since before Tink's shit got rough. I remember Tink cracking him across the face and I thought at that time he was going to hit her back. Since then he's been a total prick to just about all of us Devil's Handmaidens sisters. Well, when none of his brothers are around. With my ass burning, I hightail it after Malice and grab his arm, spinning him around. His hands automatically go up and he swings. Not bad but the dumbass must not know I've been involved with Japanese jiu-jitsu, Brazilian jiu-jitsu, along with Taekwondo, my whole adult life, since I got away from Oscar. When he tries again to swing in my direction, my many years of training kick in. I drop low so his punch misses, then I leap up and I immediately do a side kick to his family jewels, which has Malice gasping for air. Then when he's about to charge me, I hear a roar then see Malice go flying right before my eyes.

I see Enforcer with his hands around Malice's neck, squeezing tightly. Brothers come running from all directions, reaching and trying to get Enforcer off of their brother Malice, whose face is turning blue. When Yoggie gets behind Enforcer, I'm not sure what he's about to do, but when he takes his hand and squeezes right behind Enforcer's ear, the big man goes down immediately, his hands falling off his brother's neck.

Malice rolls, coughing and trying to catch his breath. When Half Pint tries to help him up, Malice pushes his hand away and struggles his way to his feet. Once he's standing, Sebastian walks up to him, grabbing him from behind, immediately strangling him. I start to scream because I couldn't give a shit about Malice but I am worried about Sebastian. His face is red and he looks like he's ready to kill the man with his bare hands. Right now, he's totally Yoggie, the one-percenter of a motorcycle club.

Moving as quickly as possible, pushing his brothers here and there, I reach Sebastian and grab his forearms.

"Sebastian, let him go. He's not worth it. Boo, you just got patched in, what do you think the Intruders will do if you kill another brother? I can tell you it won't be anything good. Let the club decide. Please, I'm begging you."

It takes a minute but it finally penetrates, and like he's coming out of a deep dream he jerks his hands away and lets Malice drop to the floor.

"Bae, you're right, but after this I'm thinking the club would have thanked me for getting rid of the trash. And you, asshole, you ever disrespect Nora again, no one will be able to save your ass. You hear me, jagoff?"

Before Malice can answer we hear boots hitting the floor and then Tank's booming voice.

"What the ever-lovin' fuck is going on? Brothers don't fight brothers unless in the ring. What's the problem, Yoggie? Malice, one of you sons of bitches better start talking, you don't want me on your ass, just sayin'."

When neither seems like they were going to tell Tank what happened, I do it.

"Just a misunderstanding, Tank. Malice seems to have a thorn under his skin for all of us Devil's Handmaidens, and not sure if it was an accident or done on purpose but he plowed into me, knocking me on my ass. Didn't seem too sorry about it either, so when I went after him. He raised fists, swung, and I finished it with a kick. Needless to say, my Boo was upset and here we are now."

"Malice, get your ass in my office now. I've had enough of your stupid kid shit. Enforcer, you okay? If so make sure he gets there, will ya? Yoggie, no fine, not gonna give ya a talking to, you just got the fuck patched in. Next time bring it to either me, Enforcer, or even Pussy if he's around. We're gonna fill the VP position soon but until then find one of us. Don't take matters in your own hands, not what this club is about. Now go grab your ol' lady and have a good night, son."

I watch my Boo's face and the look when Tank calls him son has me reaching for my chest. I know a little bit of Sebastian's past, but nothing that would put that look on his face. A look that seems to shout out with pride and joy that Tank would even consider calling him son. Going to need to start digging in and finding out more about this wonderful man.

NINE
'RAVEN'
BRENNA

My damn back is cramping up and my eyes are burning like a bitch. But when I saw this missing person report, knew I needed to follow the trail. Now I feel like Alice going down the rabbit hole. And it is all making its way around to those bastards, the Thunder Cloud Knuckle Brotherhood. I don't know why they keep bouncing in and out of all of our businesses, both personal and professional.

Just the other day one of our tractor trailers was vandalized when the driver, Joe, ran into the Wooden Spirits Bar and Grill to drop off some list from Dani that she needed to get into Taz's hands. A list of shit that was needed at the shop. By the time Joe dropped it off to Peanut, who would hand it off to Taz, and he had a cup of coffee and a bowl of soup, the entire one side of the trailer had all kinds of shit on it. And none of it was pretty, especially since right now in our country spirits our running hot. We had to have Joe bring the trailer back, unload it, and then get it cleaned off, which took a couple of hours.

How did we know it was the Thunder Cloud Knuckle Brotherhood? Well, the derogatory signs and words gave it away. And the GoPro caught two idiots leaving the scene and I was able to match them through facial recognition software I have. Dumbasses, we already called in Sheriff George so we could make a report. Taz and Tink are right, we need a paper trail to bring those sons of bitches down. Personally, I'm with Shadow, just take them down one at a time.

Hearing my alarm go off on my search computer, I turn to see what it's found. I almost fall backward when I see the picture of the little girl who's been at our ranch now for a couple of weeks. Olivia has really bonded with Glory, Taz, and Teddy. Don't forget the pups too, especially Tuna.

Diving in, I start to search who the fuck put out a missing person on that little girl. Poodles said what Olivia told us was absolutely true. Her parents were murdered and she was taken by the racist club and dropped off to Juice's in Mesquite Nevada for, as they put it, processing. What she went through has shivers going down my spine. Motherfuckers, I ever have that child tell me who I'll gladly put a bullet in their crotch first, then cut off their dick before letting them bleed to death.

But for now, all I can do is fantasize about my desire to torture these assholes. I need to let Tink and Glory know about this because it means we need to keep a close eye on Olivia now at all times. Poor kid, after all she's been through it's still not safe for her to just be a kid. Though with all of the get-togethers with Teddy, our girl Olivia is catching up for sure. And the two of them are so cute together from all the pictures Taz is sending all of us, every time they are together.

Picking up the phone, I dial up Tink's number and wait. After the second ring she picks up.

"Problem, Raven?"

I love my prez because she's always in the mix, even before I tell her anything.

"Tink, you in town? I'm at the clubhouse in my cave, need to talk to you about something important and probably pretty urgent. Don't want to talk on the cells. And just you and me to start, need to get your thoughts before we bring in any of the sisters. Especially Glory."

I can almost hear the wheels in her head turning and trying to figure out what I'm trying to tell her without the words directly. As usual, she shocks the shit outta me.

"Noodles and I are at the Wooden Spirits, had to do some inventory and he wanted lunch. Can be over in under thirty minutes, that work? And just throwing it out there, but who's it about, Olivia or Yoggie?"

Damn, how does she do this every single time? It freaks me out sometimes, well most times, if I'm being honest. Though I give it to her straight.

"Olivia, Prez."

"I'll be there shortly. You want me to bring you something to eat?"

As I tell her to bring me the special of the day with a bowl of soup, I continue to monitor my one screen as I search on the other. My third and fourth are for emergencies and to keep an eye on every camera I have out there. Alarms are set on each one and for the camera ones, I get notices for everything from motion to a person in the camera view. Can't take any chances, especially now that some of the sisters have hooked their stars and there are children involved. They are all my responsibility and I won't let them down.

* * *

Hearing the pounding on my door, I let out a scream after checking the camera on my phone to see both Tink and Noodles at my door. Great, can't even pee in private anymore.

When I open the door, both Tink and Noodles are sitting at the table with water bottles in their hands. My food has been placed on the other side and I can see from here Tink brought extra bread and butter, which are my favorites.

"Raven, sit down and eat. It can wait another five or ten minutes. We can visit, then when you're ready, you can drop the next bomb on me. Noodles is here because we drove together and as you all say, we are attached at the hip."

I chuckle as I walk to the table and take a seat. Damn, it looks so good and I'm starving. Can't remember the last time I ate a meal. Usually, I grab shit as I work.

Gotta get better at that, my mom has been riding my ass that I need to take better care of myself. Right before she tells me I need to find a man. Mothers.

Tink and I are close but nothing like she is with Shadow or Glory. I'm not upset or jealous, just thinking that's how it is in our club. Being I'm a computer nerd, can't say I'm really close with any one sister. Well, maybe Peanut and Kiwi, as we all feel like the misfits of the Devil's Handmaidens Motorcycle Club. We've gone out together and spent many nights crying on each other's shoulders about different shit that has happened in our lives. Truly though, I've been blessed, the only negative thing that has happened with my family is they aren't pleased I'm part of the club. My mom always had her dreams of her daughters finding a cowboy and getting married. Then being barefoot and pregnant just like she was. Unfortunately, that's not for me. And I found my cowboy, he just wasn't that into me.

"All right, Raven, now that we fed you and you won't pass out on me, tell me what you found. I can see by the look on your face it's not good news, for sure."

"You're right, Tink, it's not. Before I start, got to ask is it okay to discuss this in front of Noodles? Don't lose your shit, you taught me when I first took over the IT position so that's why I'm asking."

When she looks to her fiancé then back at me, I see him wink my way. Yeah, Noodles is a handful, thank God he has eyes for Tink because they are perfect together. Tink gives me the go-ahead, so I give it to her.

"All right, I've been running searches for anything

that would give me insight into that racist group that is running circles around us. From a small town on the border of Montana and Idaho, a missing child report has been filed. Yeah, you guessed it, it's for Olivia, and the report says her mother reported her missing over six months ago. I can't tell for sure by the photos, but my gut is telling me it's not her mom. Someone is playing games, and the man with the woman I was able to do facial recognition on. He's from the Thunder Cloud Knuckle Brotherhood. His name is William Johnson, he's forty-one and single. Well, maybe there isn't much on him after he got involved with the brotherhood. His mother and father were murdered. Their farm in Idaho is now a compound for the brotherhood. They train there and occasionally use it for a middle ground when trying to human traffic the victims. From his facial features he could be Olivia's father, though I believe that little girl's story about how that group killed her parents. And with those racist bastards having so many folks in their pockets, probably would be really easy to lie and say he is her father. If so, you know the courts like the kids to go to their birth family, Tink. Not sure how you want to handle this with Glory. She's gotten so attached to the girl, as Olivia has to her. For fuck's sake, they set up house in that old homestead by the pasture you had. I mean, that's what it seems like they are doing. Anyway, that's what I have for you. Tell me what you want and I'll do it, Prez, but we need to make sure Olivia is guarded and protected. If those assholes get ahold of her, she'll be gone in the blink of an eye, never to be found again."

As Tink, Noodles, and I look over what I've been able to put together, I feel like once again we are stepping into the devil's ring of fire. Even though I don't do it enough, I pray that no one gets burned this time around.

TEN
'YOGGIE'
SEBASTIAN

The itching is finally getting better. Stupid me, I picked my shoulder and mid-back for my club tattoo. I picked our club logo and behind it are trees on mountains. Seems like what I've come to love about Montana. After being in the Middle East for many years, you come to enjoy seasons, mountains, valleys, blue sky, and trees.

I've not spoken to Malice since the day he knocked Nora down, and he's never apologized. He's in huge trouble with the club because it's come to everyone's attention he's been a total dick to all of the Devil's Handmaidens sisters since the situation with Tink and Noodles. Personally, I think his manhood was threatened when tiny but mighty Tink cracked the shit outta him. And he's the type of man who would hold a grudge against a woman who was just protecting herself against a total dickhead.

Getting my head outta my own ass, I concentrate on the road as I make my way to Taz and Enforcer's house.

Olivia spent the day with Teddy and I'm picking her up on my way to Nora's house. Well, she keeps saying it's our home, but I'm not sure it is. Something is eating at my gut and I don't have a fucking clue what.

There are times I feel like someone is watching me, but when I look around I don't see a thing. Also, along with Nora, I'm getting calls and hang-ups. It freaked out Olivia the other night when both of our phones rang at the same time and when we answered, we both lost our shit in our own way, and Olivia lost her shit. She ran and hid in her closet, all the way in the back. When we finally got her out and calmed down and to bed, Nora and I talked, both agreeing we have to be more careful around her. That poor kid has been through enough, we don't need to add to her troubles.

We also both agreed to have Olivia start therapy with the new doc at the Blue Sky Sanctuary. She's been coming to the ranch once or twice a week to meet with the folks on the waitlist for the sanctuary. She also works with the survivors the Devil's Handmaidens bring back from each human trafficking circuit they bust. Finally, Cynthia, the former bank manager, and her kids are also in therapy and can't say enough about Joan. Again, Cynthia's another woman, that the Thunder Cloud Knuckle Brotherhood destroyed just because they could. Proud though that she's fighting her way back.

I park off to the side so if anyone needs to get into their garage they can. I hate being in my cage, but Miss Olivia is worth it. That little girl has wormed her way deep into my heart. I can't believe how much she's drawn me out, just by being so cute and innocent. Even with the abuse she's suffered at the hands of the brotherhood, Olivia is trying to move forward. With that thought, she still wakes up in the middle of the night screaming. The first time, we ran out of the bedroom with Nora and I both butt-ass naked, each of us holding a gun in one hand. I almost showed the girl my shit and am sure that would have probably scarred her worse than she already is. Nora pulled me back, gun in one hand, robe on her naked body.

So deep in my thoughts, I don't hear the door open but feel a kind of calm feeling in the air as I walk up the stairs. Looking up, I see Cynthia Mick's son, Benji, watching me intently. Sometimes this boy seems to always be taking shit in and doesn't talk too much. Kind of reminds me of the son of Stitch in the Grimm Wolves MC.

"Hey, Benji, how's things going today? The brats behave?"

He tilts his head one way then the other before he gives me a grin.

"Yoggie, you're funny, man. Olivia and Teddy are planning their wedding as we speak. They are so serious and all they talk about is being in love. Taz tries to explain that they are too young to be in love. Teddy threw a fit, telling his mom that he supported her when she *'got together and was making kissy faces'* with Enforcer, and she needs to support him with Olivia. I had to go to the bathroom, so no one got mad, I was laughing so dang hard. Not sure how Enforcer can sit in there, but he manages. Think it's because Taz is always cracking jokes. Wanted to tell you something before you go in, you know, man-to-man."

Now it's my turn to tilt my head and stare at him. Man-to-man, what the hell is he talking about? I feel a tinge of nerves running up and down my back but I say nothing, just wait.

"Yoggie, I need to warn you. Talked to my mom, you know, Cynthia and she said to do what I thought was right, and this feels right. Don't ask questions please, just listen. Olivia is having more nightmares and she seems to be blanking out sometimes. And she's really afraid of the dark. I wasn't going to tell, but Mom said she'll try and talk to Glory in the morning when she checks in at the bunkhouse. Just want you to know that the brotherhood is everywhere."

With that, he turns and goes back in the front door, passing Enforcer on the way. I stare at him knowing there is shock all over my face. I have no idea how to process what just happened. When Enforcer walks down the stairs, grabbing my shoulders and turning me toward the outbuilding, I follow. He says not a word until we are behind closed doors and he's reset the alarm.

"Yoggie, what I'm about to tell you is for your ears only. Not even Glory can know at this snapshot in time. Got it, brother?"

I nod and wait.

"Freak found some shit out and right now we have no fuckin' solid proof, but seems like one of the brothers has some distant ties to that messed-up brotherhood. No not gonna give you a name or anything else. Just know we have your back, along with your ol' lady and kid. I know Benji told you that your girl is having nightmares, and she is. They are getting worse and that could be because of the therapy. It brings everything someone's gone through to the surface. Yeah, I know what I'm talking about. Taz, Teddy, and I met with the new doctor, Joan, when all that shit went down with my ol' lady. Fingers crossed, you and Glory can get by without too much drama. Now let's get inside before someone has another meltdown. Teddy is driving us crazy with his idea that him and Olivia will be getting married later in the year. Olivia doesn't say much but smiles every time he says anything about their 'relationship.' I know she was having a pretty intense conversation with Que today about relationships. She seemed worried as she told my ol' lady Teddy might not want her if he found out about what happened at that house she was held in. My woman told her any man worthy of her wouldn't let anything from the past stop his love for her. Olivia seemed to like that answer. Now, brother, let's get our asses in there before one or all of those monsters come out wanting to play hide-and-seek, or worse, want to go pet all the animals up at the ranch. Again."

Laughing along with Enforcer, we make our way up the porch and through the front door. I stop immediately when I see Teddy holding on to a crying Olivia while Benji and Dakota stand close by. Taz is on her knees next to the kids, rubbing up and down Olivia's back. When she sees us walk in she gives Enforcer big eyes. I walk directly to the little girl, and when she sees me, she lets go of Teddy and walks to me, arms up in the air for me to pick her up. When I do, she puts her head on my shoulder and holds on tightly.

"Que, what the hell happened? I was gone maybe eight to ten minutes. What's the drama now?"

Teddy turns around, his eyes first on me then his dad. He walks over to Enforcer pulling on his kutte to get him to come down to his level. Teddy does his whisper, which isn't a whisper at all.

"Daddy, we've got a problem. Momma was on the house phone with Miss Cynthia, making sure that Benji and Dakota could stay for dinner and maybe watch a movie. Momma's cell phone rang. I was in the bathroom, and Benji and Dakota were playing with Tuna, Atticus, and Skylar. Olivia was trying to be helpful and when she answered the phone, whoever was on it said something that totally freaked her out, Dad. She started to scream, making Momma drop the phone to see what was wrong. By the time I got out into the room, Olivia was crying and shaking. She ran to me so I held her like you always hold my momma. That's what you guys walked into. Momma tried but can't get anything out of Olivia about who was on the phone, or what they said to make her so upset."

Before Enforcer or I can say a word, we hear footsteps running up the stairs and we both move outta the way as the door opens and Nora, Shadow, and

Raven come in the door looking frantic. Nora comes to Olivia and me, putting her hands on the little girl's back.

"Cariño, Taz called, said you were upset by a phone call. What's going on, Olivia? You know you can trust Yoggie and me. Well, you can trust everyone in this room. No one will let anyone or anything hurt you, ever. I promised you on our way back here that I'd protect you, but need to know, honey, what's got you so upset. Please, Olivia, talk to us."

Olivia picks her head up off my shoulder then looks between me and my Bae. She reaches one hand out to touch Nora's face, then brings that hand to my face. Her little face is pink and wet with her tears.

"Glory, I answered Miss Taz's phone and the voice told me to *'enjoy your time there'* because it was going to come to an end soon. Told me I was going to live with my new mommy and daddy. The voice told me I already know my daddy because we met at that bad house. That made me scream. My heart was beating really hard too. Please don't let any of those bad, mean men take me. Please."

My eyes immediately go to Nora's, and I make a promise to myself that no one, and I mean no one, will ever hurt Nora or Olivia ever again if I can help it.

ELEVEN
'GLORY'
NORA

After eating dinner at Taz and Enforcer's, the kids watched a movie while all the adults sat on the back deck, trying to figure out who the hell would try to scare our little girl. Something isn't right, and by the way Raven ran after Shadow and me when I got the call, figure she's working every angle possible. Those motherfuckers in the brotherhood have their hands in just about every deviant action out there. And for some reason everything we are involved in leads right back to them. I know Tink and Tank have been having conversations, trying to figure out how both clubs are tied to this racist group of assholes. Well, besides when Taz had her drama and the Grimm Wolves and Tank decided to blow up the brotherhood's compound.

By the time we left, Sebastian had to carry Olivia to my car because she was totally out. Little Teddy got mad because he told Sebastian he would carry our girl out, but when he tried to he couldn't lift her. He got so mad tears started to roll down his cheeks. Leave it to my Boo to make him feel better.

"Teddy, my man, don't get upset. Right now you're helping Olivia much more by being her friend. One day you'll be the only man picking her up, but for now, be thankful you have your dad and all of his brothers to step up to the plate 'til you get bigger. Remember that being a man isn't about how strong you are but being a good man, and more importantly, a good human being in all ways. You're on the road for that, so just keep doing what you're doing. So gotta ask you, my man, may I carry your ol' lady out to the car?"

I was watching Teddy's face as Sebastian talked to him and he actually ended up smiling while wiping his tears off his face. His smile was huge when my Boo called Olivia his ol' lady. I almost busted a gut, but did my best not to even smile as Teddy was in a very sensitive mood and didn't want him to think I was laughing at him. We all learned that when he is having a moment to just support him emotionally, so he doesn't draw into himself like he used to do when Taz first came into the Devil's Handmaidens. It helped that his favorite auntie was there. Never got how close Teddy and Shadow are, but hey, who am I to judge. They say kids are a good judge of character. Even though Shadow tries to scare the shit out of everyone she has a very good heart, especially for those she cares about.

So while Sebastian carries Olivia out, Shadow makes it a point to hold Teddy's hand as they both follow us out to my vehicle. He leans in and puts a soft kiss on her cheek before I shut the back door. Teddy then comes right up to me and gives me a tight hug.

"Auntie Glory, thanks for bringing Olivia home to us. I promise to take care of her, just like all the men take care of their ol' ladies. Won't let anything happen to her. See you tomorrow."

Then he takes Shadow's hand and goes to walk back to the house. Shadow leans down and says something to him that has him letting her hand go and run to the house by himself. My sister comes toward us and by the intensity of those ice-blue eyes of hers, I know whatever she is going to say, I won't like.

"Glory, wasn't going to tell ya, but with this, figure you should know, though we don't have much yet. Raven found some bullshit report that someone is looking for Olivia and has a missing person report filed. They say they are her parents. And we both know that's a fuckin' lie, sister, because little Olivia told all of us those bastards killed her parents and took her to that hell she was living in. Raven went as deep as she could without them finding out she's looking into them. The guy claiming to be her father is, in fact, part of the Thunder Cloud Knuckle Brotherhood. In fact, his dad is a founding member of the Timber-Ghost chapter, I guess you'd call it. So this jagoff grew up in that brotherhood and has probably been brainwashed. Glory, we got this, don't lose your goddamn mind 'cause no one can get on the ranch or by any of the homesteads. We made sure of that after all the other sisters' dramas. Go home, get some sleep, we'll talk in the morning."

Then she blew my mind by giving me a quick hug. After, she turned and walked back to the house. Sebastian is waiting by the driver's side with the door open. Knowing he won't leave until I'm in safe and sound in my cage, I walk over to him. He grabs me close, giving me a hard, closed-mouth kiss before he helps me into the driver's seat. After I start my car, I wait for him to get in his cage then follow him home. My mind is going in all directions because I can feel deep in my gut that shit is about to go to hell. All I can pray for is, no matter what comes our way, we can keep Olivia safe and make sure nothing more happens to her. She's gone through enough.

* * *

By the time we get back to the house and I get Olivia out of her clothes and into her jammies, she is wide awake. She wants both of us to read her a story, so Sebastian and I do just that. By the time we were halfway through she is out again. We finish the story then tuck her in, turn her stars motion light on, and shut the door only partway. She can't be in the dark or locked in or she freaks out. Some nights, lately, she wakes up either screaming or crying.

I'm exhausted but need to take a quick shower. Looking for Sebastian, I find him in the kitchen making a sandwich.

"Boo, I'm going to jump in the shower. You okay? Keep an ear out for Olivia, will you please?"

"Bae, you don't have to ask, for Christ's sake, just go take five minutes for yourself. I'll be right here when you're done. Want me to make you a sandwich?"

Nodding, I turn and walk back to our bedroom and the bathroom. Turning on the shower to warm up, I start to take my clothes off then step into the shower. Once the water hits me, I feel it building, and before I can stop it, my emotions go into overload. Between the water and tears running down my face, everything hits me at once. I lean against the tile wall, head hanging, and just let everything out. Not sure how long I'm in here before I feel arms wrapping around me and my Boo pulls me up tightly, my back to his front. He doesn't say a word, just holds me closely, which is exactly what I need in this moment. Feeling safe is something that is hard for me to feel. Even now.

Not sure how much time goes by before his hands start to caress my belly, but he never goes up or down. He's comforting me. This man is beyond perfect. The more his hands are on me, the tingling feelings are growing. My body is relaxed while my mind has quieted down. When his fingers slip below my tummy, I feel all my muscles tense as his long, rough fingers make their way down to my lady bits. Just that thought has me giggling because that's what Raven is always saying.

"Bae, I'm afraid to ask what's so funny. Not exactly the reaction I

was looking for when my hands are on you. Gasps, moans, whimpers, or crying out my name, or even Oh my Gods, but not giggles. Woman, no man wants that. So do I want to know or not?"

"Boo, it's not you. As you were traveling south, I heard Raven's voice and how she calls where you were going lady bits. It made me giggle, but swear it wasn't about you or what you were doing. In fact, you can get back to it anytime you want. I'm waiting impatiently, Sebastian."

His fingers are on the move again. When his rough fingertips find my hidden bundle of nerves, I take in a deep breath.

"Breathe, Bae. I got ya."

And man, does he have me. Between his fingers and mouth, the sounds coming from me surprise me. I just try to breathe and enjoy and feel what he's doing to me. It's all about me every time, and that alone makes me feel so special. The build keeps coming until I can't hold back. My body lets go and Sebastian holds on to me until I'm limp and feeling beyond relaxed. He then moves me under the water and washes every inch of me, including shampooing my hair. Having those fingers on my scalp, lightly scrubbing, has goosebumps rising all up and down my arms. When he rinses out the conditioner, he turns me, placing a gentle kiss on my lips, then kisses my nose.

After he turns the shower off, he reaches out, grabbing a towel that he wraps my hair in. The next towel he dries me off in the shower before wrapping me in it.

"Bae, go on to bed. I'll just be a minute, want to take

a quick one. I'll check on Olivia when I'm done. Go take care of you for a change."

My body feels like I'm floating as I make my way to the bedroom. Dropping the towel, I reach under my pillow, pulling out the huge nightshirt I sleep in. Moving to my dresser, I grab a pair of my boxers and pull them up. Knowing I'll have a mess in the morning, I skip drying my hair but drop that towel also and finger brush my hair before pulling the covers back and getting into bed.

Hearing the shower turn off, I shift, trying to get comfortable as I hear Sebastian enter the bedroom. He grabs his sleep shorts then leaves, probably to check on Olivia. I'm drifting off as he makes his way back and into bed. He pulls me close, his nose in my hair.

"Bae, sleep good, beautiful. Tomorrow will be a better day, promise. I got you, Nora, always."

This is the last thing I hear before I fall deeply asleep and don't wake up until the sun is already in the sky.

TWELVE
'YOGGIE'
SEBASTIAN

I have to bring Tank into this bullshit that is starting to escalate. He needs to know, but more importantly, I need the Intruders at my back guarding my family. I don't think I'd be able to survive if something ever happened to Nora or Olivia. As one of my foster dads used to say sarcastically, I tend to lead with my heart. With Nora, she took my breath away the first time I saw her. Now that I've had her, not going anywhere. She's it for me.

Knocking on the front door of Tank and Momma Diane's house, I hear the dogs start to go crazy. Checking my watch, to make sure I'm not too early, the door flings open and Momma Diane is there staring at me before a wide smile appears on her face. She pulls me in and gives me a huge hug before she smiles wide.

"Yoggie, Tank told me you and Glory are together. That really warms my heart. That child needs someone in her life."

"Momma Diane, I agree. Olivia needs stable folks around her so she can eventually move past all that bullshit and just live a good life."

"Son, I wasn't talking about Olivia, though she needs family too. I was referring to Glory. That girl has been living in a jail cell since she came here from out East. Yeah, she's my daughter's right hand, but she needs someone special in her life. Is that you, Yoggie?"

Before I can answer, I hear him before I see him.

"Woman, mind your own damn business. And you wonder why I don't share shit with ya. If our girl, Glory, was to hear you had cornered her ol' man, shit would be flyin'. Come on in, Yoggie. We just started our morning coffee, so come get a cup. Then we can hit my home office and you can tell me what you need. Now get, woman, I'm in need of breakfast."

I grin at their constant give and take. That right there is what I want with Nora, but it's gonna take time. Especially after what she shared with me about her past. One day at a time is all we can do. For now, gonna enjoy this time with these two people, who embody what family really means and how important it is in our lives.

Sitting in Tank's office with my third cup of coffee after a delicious breakfast Momma Diane whipped up, I'm trying to figure out how to explain to Tank my concerns and what I'm asking for.

"Brother, just spit it out. Don't even give it any thought 'cause that's when shit gets confusing and complicated. There ain't nothin' you can say to me that would shock me, or even worse, make me look at you differently. Yoggie, since you've started, your only thoughts were about our club and each and every brother. You need to understand that as an Intruder it's a two-way street. What you put out there is returned back to you. So, give it to me so we can figure out how we move forward."

Taking a deep breath, I start to explain to my president why I'm beyond concerned with what my ol' lady shared with me a couple of days ago. The worst part is that her brother-in-law, Oscar, has connections with the Thunder Cloud Knuckle Brotherhood. When she explained that, I had a bad feeling go down my spine. Those motherfuckers are like a bad penny, for Christ's sake. Between our club and Nora's, they keep popping into our view and lives.

Tank sits at his home desk, not saying a word while I speak. When I finally finish with a plea for added protection for both Nora and Olivia, he tilts his head at me for a minute or so.

"Son, you got it bad, don't ya? My girl Glory better realize how lucky she is that you're in her life. Now give me a minute, will ya? No, ya don't have to leave, just take a breath will you?"

I watch as he reaches over, grabbing his phone, and dialing but I don't have a clue who. Well, until he starts talking.

"Enforcer, yeah, brother, morning to you too. Need ya to get up to the main house as quick as possible. Put a shout out to Pussy and Freak, as I need to have a word with all three of you. No, it's not bad but more of a warning, and thank God we're getting it. Also, I'm gonna call in my daughters Tink, Shadow, and Glory. We've got a situation brewing and we need to get in front of it. Yeah, thanks, brother. Oh, I hear my little man, give Teddy a hug from his grandpa. Tell him I'll see him soon and we'll go, just the two of us, to the Wooden Spirits Bar and Grill for lunch and an ice cream sundae for dessert."

"Yoggie, don't worry, which I can't believe I just said that shit, must be lack of something this morning. So, while we wait for our brothers to get their asses here, give me the gossip of whatever ya know. That woman of mine keeps all the good shit to herself nowadays."

As we sit and shoot the shit, I'm so grateful I literally bumped into Enforcer when my head was up my ass after my last mission that fucked me up. I've done all the therapy, both physically and mentally, and have to say being a part of the Intruders has been more help than any of the rest. Yeah, it's hard and trying, but I'd not change it for anything. I've got a family that was missing in my life.

Sometimes it's hard to swallow some of the shit we do, just because for the first part of my life I was all about my country and doing what was right. Though I learned the hard way what you might think you're doing is right, it can go to shit in a quick minute. Our club's mission in the long run is to protect the innocent. Seems, even though some of our work is on the other side of the law, it's only to achieve our goal of protecting those who can't protect themselves. Tank is learning from his daughter and her club in regard to the sick and demented in this world of ours. On the top of that list is that brotherhood. We need to put them all to ground, and soon.

The knock on the door draws our attention as Intruder, Freak, and Pussy stroll in, smirks on their faces until they see ours. Then the three of them are on alert. It's like they can read the air in the room. As Tank starts to explain the situation, I feel eyes on me. When I look around it's Intruder who's giving me the eye. I raise my one eyebrow, which he smirks at. When Tank is done, the room is quiet for a minute then Freak jumps in.

"I'll try to get a bead on her husband and daughter. Hey, no disrespect, Yoggie, just sayin' what I'm gonna be looking into. Also, I'll try to get updated information on the asshole brother-in-law in the can. Will keep all of you updated. Is this to be kept under wraps right now?"

Tank looks at me and I give him a nod, which he relays to Freak. He gets up and walks out. Pussy stands and starts toward the door before he turns around and takes us in.

"I get the feeling until we fuckin' end the Thunder Cloud Knuckle Brotherhood this shit is gonna keep bogging us down. And what the fuck kind of name is that anyway? Dumb motherfuckers, couldn't they come up with a badass name that would put fear in folks' hearts? I mean Thunder Cloud Knuckle Brotherhood sounds like a misfit band of grown Boy Scouts, for Christ's sake."

Tank, Intruder, and I look at each other for less than

five seconds before we all start laughing. Our brother Pussy always has a way with words, that's for sure. Before he can open the door to leave, someone knocks—no, pounds—on the door before it swings open and I see Tink and Shadow first, but then between them I see Nora. I told her what I was up to this morning, but she still seems surprised to see me sitting in Tank's office.

"Pops, you called?"

Shadow is grinning as Tink growls that to her dad. Bet there has been some intense shit between those three, just by the vibe in the room. As Intruder pulls three chairs from the table in the corner, Momma Diane shows up with a tray of coffee and some morning pastries, which the women fall on immediately. Fuck, they are like rabid starving dogs, for God's sake. I know Nora ate because I made her breakfast before I left. Both her and Olivia. It was the little one's day to pick and she wanted pancakes.

Tank waits 'til everyone is seated again and Pussy shuts the door when he finally leaves. No one says a word for a bit until Nora looks at me.

"Sebastian, you weren't lying when you said this morning during breakfast you'd be reaching out to Tank. I had no idea that would be the first thing on your agenda though."

"Bae, you're always the first thing on my agenda, every single day."

I hear both Tink and Shadow sigh as Intruder chokes on his coffee. Tank just smirks. I don't care what anyone thinks, not going to play games with Nora now that everyone knows we are together. Life is way too fuckin' short.

When everything calms down, Tank goes over what I told him, asking Nora questions here and there. Everyone listens as she goes through her past, taking in what she's not saying. When Tank finishes, Intruder jumps in.

"I've had extra eyes on Que and Teddy since all our shit went down. We can rotate some of the prospects to include you, Glory, and Olivia. Now, don't get your shit in an uproar, been there with Que, it aint' gonna make a difference. Do you know what kind of man you hooked your star to? Yeah, I said it. He's one of us and we take care of our own, just like y'all take care of us. That's what happens when you're in a *'grown-up'* relationship. Now, Prez, I'll get a schedule together. Glory, try to keep Olivia with Teddy as much as possible. Yeah, I know that won't be a problem. Last night my son asked me to be his best man at their wedding. And no, I didn't argue with him about being too young and shit. Que told me not to because Teddy gets all upset, and we don't want to set him into an autistic episode. I'll let Que know and if you two can hang together, that'd be great. I hired a few of Ollie's folks to keep an eye on my family from a distance. Que wasn't happy, but they are ex-military so I feel a bit better knowing they have some extra protection, just in case."

With that, between our two biker families I feel a bit less stress, knowing everyone is on the same page and both Nora and Olivia have extra eyes on them. Feeling hands on my waist, I look down into Nora's beautiful eyes that are shining.

"Thanks, Sebastian, for caring so much. It's a new feeling for me to have a man who cares enough to make sure I'm protected, though I can take care of myself. Remember, I'm a black belt in multiple disciplines. I want you to know how much I appreciate you making sure Olivia is safe because she needs to feel that for the rest of her life."

Then she lifts up and kisses me with all that she's feeling. We hang on to each other until, at the same time, both Shadow and Intruder tell us to get a room while Tink and Tank laugh.

Good start to our day for sure.

THIRTEEN
'RAVEN'
BRENNA

Fuck, I need to start exercising or eating less. All these hours on my ass with limited movement have me in extreme pain everywhere. All my muscles are tightening while my back and neck are cramping constantly. I need a good massage to get loose since I ain't got a man to do it. Might need to talk to Heartbreaker or Duchess to see where they go for theirs. Both of those sisters bring bougie to another level. Well, for sure Heartbreaker, though she's kinda calmed down after her last relapse. Now that sister is always around to lend a hand or take on the worst jobs possible. Even worse than the prospects, which is saying a lot.

Searching for ghosts is not my favorite thing to do. Glory's husband and daughter disappeared off the face of the earth the day that dick Oscar walked away with Glory. Though she never has gone into much detail about it to me, I've done some background on that asshole and, man, he's a sadist to the maximum.

Before he even fixated on Glory, he was accused of multiple domestics and two rapes but no one ever pressed charges. Well, out of the four times cops were called in, two of the victims just disappeared, never to be seen again. The other two just out of the blue dropped the charges, not wanting anything to do with Oscar. So that tells me someone got in their faces. Victim harassment. And for that to happen, Oscar had to call someone or ones to have his back. All fingers are pointing to our nemesis, the Thunder Cloud Knuckle Brotherhood. Diving in, I can see a connection between the brotherhood and Glory's brother-in-law Oscar. They were in business together; I just don't know what kind yet. I'm sure though it's illegal.

I've traced back some disappearances that tie both Oscar and the brotherhood together, though there is no solid proof that either are involved, just circumstantial evidence, which doesn't help at all.

I also checked with the prison and supposedly Oscar is still incarcerated, but need to talk to Tink and Tank because I got a weird feeling talking to that administrator on the phone. Just when I go to pick it up my cell rings, which freaks me out. I hate when that happens. Looking at the screen, I see Freak's name so I grab it.

"What's up, fellow nerd?"

"Raven, where are you? I need your help and I mean now."

"Calm the hell down, Freak. I'm at the clubhouse in my office. What's got your balls in a sling today?"

"Tank has me looking into your sister, Glory, and her history. I think I found something but don't want to go off half-cocked before I have confirmation. I've tried a few things but not gettin' what I want. Think you can help me?"

"Sure, come on by. I'll let whoever is up front know to let you in, just come to my office. It won't be open, as you know, so knock your knock and I'll let ya in. How long before ya get here?'

Listening to Freak, he tells me no longer than twenty to thirty minutes. Knowing him like I do, probably should cut that in half. Once we hang up, I look through my contacts, find the one I want, and hit it.

"Heartbreaker, hey, sister, it's me. Freak is on his way so let him in and send him back. Would you mind maybe brewing some coffee and, I don't know, those wraps you make? I'm sure the bastard will be starving. And remember no matter how much he begs, no energy drinks. I don't care if he begs or offers to pay you, just say no. Thanks, appreciate it, Heartbreaker."

While I wait, I continue to scan through anything related to that crazy as fuck brotherhood. I'm looking at pictures taken of different compounds and shit monkey balls, I literally freeze. Holy shit, mother of God, how can that be? What the fuck am I looking at? On the screen is a teenage girl who could pass as Glory's doppelgänger. No way, this can't be? How and why would that kid be with those assholes? I thought Glory said when she married Gino he was the good one in the family. Why then would their daughter be hanging out at one of the Thunder Cloud Knuckle Brotherhood's compounds? Especially since Oscar has ties to them?

I grab that photo and get to work. My computer is scanning documents and photos at such a fast rate I can't even make out what it's going through. I coded this program myself to find either documents or photos with the specific parameters. I start to gather the documents lying all over to put in my desk safe, when my computer starts pinging. Then picture after picture appears on the screen. Motherfucker, it's like a picture book of Glory's daughter Lilly's life. Opening the safe that looks like a file cabinet, I toss everything in, even though our club trusts Freak we don't trust him one-hundred-percent. And him being in Tank's club doesn't make us believe he's all in. There are very few who the Devil's Handmaidens consider family to our club. That handful includes Panther, Avalanche, Noodles, Ollie, Intruder, Dr. Cora, and Cynthia who was working really hard and was on her way, earning our trust slowly.

Hearing Freak's knock at my door—the hard knock, soft knock, then a rap—I get up and with my gun at my side look through the computer, showing me who's out there. And it's Freak making a face at the door, which means he's assuming there is a camera. Fucking dork is too smart for his own britches. I unlatch the door and he walks in with his laptop, tablet, and a folder filled with papers. One glance at my screen that I forgot to minimize and he flips out.

"What the fuck, Raven? You know already and

didn't share with me? Not good, sister. Here I thought I found gold and you've been sittin' on it. Goddamn it."

"Sit the fuck down, Freak, and shut it. I just ran across this and was in the middle of a face detection search when you got here. So, let's start at the beginning. Apparently, you also found this, right? And you, like me, are guessing this might be Lilly, Glory's missing daughter. So come on, tell me what else you got so we can compare notes."

Right when he starts another knock comes at the door. He lets out a snarl while I flip him off, knowing it's Heartbreaker. She has the code but probably has her hands full with food and coffee, so I open up. And she has a huge tray covered with shit.

"Come on in, sister. Put it on that table, if ya don't mind."

Freak jumps up, immediately grabbing the tray from Heartbreaker but not meeting her eyes. I look at her and she gives me big eyes. What the fuck is his problem? Before I can say a word, he looks up, face a slight pink.

"Hey, Heartbreaker, how's it goin'? Thanks for this, I'm starving. Hey, do you got any energy drinks by chance, forgot to bring one?"

She angles toward me, giving me a look I don't know. Then I see in her kutte pocket, a can hanging out. Oh, no fucking way, I told her not to. Before I can say a word, I catch the way she's looking at him. Are these two together? Since when? And of course my mouth runs away before I can think.

"Oh my Lord, are you two freaks bumping nasties?

When did this shit even start? I thought you lived in front of the computer, Freak, and, Heartbreaker, you hate computers. Come on, someone start talking. What? Cat got your tongues, for Christ's sake."

Heartbreaker turns bright red to match her hair but says not a word. She reaches inside her kutte, grabbing a can of—oh shit—Coke and hands it to Freak. His eyes are looping around the room, but not once does he look Heartbreaker in the eyes. My sister turns to leave then stops and looks at the two of us.

"Raven, no, Freak and I aren't bumping anything. We barely even know each other and after this he'll probably not ever want to see or talk to me again. Sorry about her, Freak, she's got no filter or, at times, common sense, though she's smart as can be. If either of you need anything, just call me."

With that she leaves, shutting the door behind her. I hear Freak let out a deep breath so I turn to see he's staring at the door, looking like a lost puppy. Damn it, I jumped the gun. My matchmaking skills must be off today. When Freak looks my way, I'm stunned. He looks shocked.

"Never thought she'd even look my way. Fuck, with all the other brothers around who are bigger, stronger, and look better than I'll ever look, didn't think I had a chance. Son of a bitch, I've got a chance, don't I, Raven? If I wasn't in here with you, I'd do a dance or kick my heels up. But we got work to do, so I'll push this awesome feeling to the side for the time being. Oh, thanks for that, Raven, you opened a door. I was too chickenshit to even try to touch the fuckin' handle. Now back to this shit, that's gotta be Glory's kid, right? So if she is, where the hell is Glory's husband, and the million-dollar question is why are they with that brotherhood? That's what we need to dig up because without that we won't get any answers. So let's put our heads together and get the answers so we can take them to Glory, Tank, and Tink."

With that he grabs a wrap, taking a huge bite. He pops the tab on his Coke—swallowing a quarter of the can—then whips out his laptop, flipping it open, and I watch as his fingers fly across the keys. I think to myself, *what the fuck just happened?* Then I grab a wrap, starting to eat as I look through the pictures on my screen, trying to find anything that would lead us to where this young woman is being held, I'm assuming, and more importantly, why.

Looking at Freak then back at my computer, I can just feel this is going to be one long-ass day. Just what my aching back needs. NOT!

FOURTEEN
'GLORY'
NORA

Not sure what the hell is going on, but Raven told me it's extremely important and urgent that I get, in her words, *'my fine ass'* to her office in the clubhouse. So once again I'm getting ready to jump in my cage to go meet her, then on the way back I'll pick up Olivia from Taz's.

Then I hear the roar of pipes that seem to be coming my way. When I see the group of bikes, I know this has something to do with what Raven wants me in her office for. I see Tink, then Shadow, Rebel, and bringing up the rear is Enforcer, Sebastian, and who the fuck is that? Must be one of the newest prospects I've not met yet.

I walk to the middle of our front yard and wait. When they all circle me in, they turn their bikes off but remain sitting on them. Well, everyone except Sebastian, who gets off and walks directly to me, pulling me close. Now I'm starting to worry. What the hell has everyone freaked out?

"Ride with me, Bae."

"What's going on, Boo? Why are all of you here and why does Raven want me to rush to her office?"

"Do you trust me, Nora? If you do, ride with me and you'll get your answers. Otherwise, get in your cage and follow your sisters."

He didn't say it but I heard what he didn't say. If I don't ride with him, he won't be with me. That scares the hell out of me, so I walk to my cage, open the trunk, and grab a coat. Putting it on, I walk back to Sebastian and he puts his arm out for me. I grab it and lift up onto the back of his bike. All at once they start their bikes up and, in a line, we ride out of our driveway, heading toward our town, Timber-Ghost.

At first, I think it is the cool air and from being on the back of a bike, but then the trembling begins. Sebastian puts his left hand on my calf, squeezing it, letting me know he's there. Running through everything in my head, I can't fathom what it could be that has everyone up in arms, so to speak. Unless, oh God, could Oscar have gotten out of jail and no one notified me? I grab on to Sebastian tighter and place my head on his kutte, praying that out of everything my thoughts aren't right. The thought of that monster back on the streets turns my stomach. We have no idea everything he was into before he lost his mind and attacked my family and took me, where I spent over two years living in his hell.

There isn't a day that goes by that Lilly and Gino don't have a place in my heart and, more importantly, in my thoughts. Sometimes I wonder what happened to the two of them. Other times, I hate to say it, try to forget they even existed because then maybe it won't hurt as bad still. Even with how full my life is, there is a part of my heart that will never heal. I lost my first love and husband, my lovely innocent daughter, and my baby, all because one man was fucking insane. I can't go back to visit my family because it tears my heart out when I see places we went to as a family. Last time we did a ride out to the Devil's Handmaidens Atlantic City Chapter, as thrilled as I was to see my sisters Harlow, Pepper and Momma, everywhere we went I was looking for Gino and Lilly, but worse I was scanning to see if Oscar was watching me again. I told Harlow then I'd probably not make the trip again, so she told me it just gives her a reason to jump on her bike and ride out to Montana.

Besides this, the other thing that comes to mind is maybe it's the brotherhood again. We need to figure out a way to take them down, once and for all. They have so many ties to very important and powerful people in this country that we don't know the first thing about. With my mind all over the damn place, I'm shocked when we pull down the road to our clubhouse. Sebastian again puts his arm out for me to dismount. Once off, I wait 'til everyone has parked and are all standing together. Tink comes toward me then grabs me, pulling me close to her. I feel her grab my kutte to pull her tiny self up to me.

"Glory, no matter what the fuck is going on, remember one thing always. I have your back, as do all the Devil's Handmaidens sisters, including our prospects. We'll figure it out, so please don't forget that. Now, let's get this shit done."

With that she opens the door and we all head inside. Sebastian is hanging on to my hand and that alone gives me some comfort. That is until I see who else is already in our common/party room. Tank, Noodles, Panther, Avalanche, and Ollie, who has a couple of his people—including Phantom and Bloody Mary—or I guess should call her Spirit as that's the name she gave to Shadow. Also, a couple of others I don't recognize. Damn, why do we need all these folks here? I have no idea.

Sebastian and I follow Tink and Shadow down the corridor not to Tink's office, but I'm guessing to Raven's. Shadow pounds first then scans her eye before putting her left hand on the pad. The door clicks then opens. This office is pretty big, but not with all the people filing in. We are the last to squeeze in, and when I look around, I see Heartbreaker and Freak here too. Well fuck, I was gonna ask what the ever-lovin' fuck is going on but I hear Tank clear his throat. Enforcer let's out his piercing whistle and the room goes an eerie quiet. When it's silent, Tank starts in.

"All right, let's dive right in. Everyone kinda knows Glory's story and if ya don't, it's hers to speak about, so if she's not shared, she probably thinks it's not your business. Now, everyone knows that Raven and Freak have been working on a special project for both my daughter and me. Glory, I think you're probably the only one who doesn't know about this project. I need you to try and stay calm now, please. Let me finish before you lose your shit and, believe me, I know you're gonna lose it. Their main objective is to locate Gino and Lilly. One or both, we needed to find out first if they were alive and, second, where they were. Today, Raven then Freak came upon some footage from the Thunder Cloud Knuckle Brotherhood. Now this is from multiple compounds, but they each found something that made them look harder. Then they got together and dug deeper. And what they found just about knocked us outta our shoes. Calm down, Glory, told you not sharin' 'til you're calm. And believe me, I know how hard it is to be calm."

I watch as Tank's eyes flip to Tink and Shadow. I feel a shift as the door opens wide and I see every Devil's Handmaidens sister in the hallway with stoic, serious faces. Oh God, please don't let this be something like Taz or Vixen just went through. Don't think I'll be able to make it if another drama is about to unfold. Sebastian lets my hand go and pulls me into him so our fronts are touching everywhere. The room goes eerily quiet as he gently lifts my chin with two fingers. When he places his lips on mine, it's not a hot and heavy kiss or a quick see ya later one. This one means something and I can't figure out what. When he finally lifts up, he stares at me for a minute before he whispers for my ears only.

"Bae, remember we are in this together. I'll be here until I die or you kick my ass to the curb. In a minute I'm gonna have you turn around and look Raven's way. I want you to be aware that I'll be right behind you, so if you need anything at all, reach behind you, that's where my ass will be. Ready?"

"For fuck's sake, Boo, I have no idea what's about to happen. You are all freaking the shit out of me. Just get it over with, will you, Sebastian? The suspense is giving me a damn ulcer."

Slowly he lets me go and turns me to face the room. At first it doesn't register but when it does, my heart feels like it cracks right down the middle in my chest. On every screen there are pictures of a young girl, all different ages. The most recent are on the center computer screen, and there is no doubt who she is. I mean, I feel like I'm looking in a mirror at my younger self. I just don't understand how, so I ask.

"How did you find her and where is she? Come on, I'm going insane here, people. Where the fuck is my daughter, Lilly, and why didn't some of you go get her and bring her here? I can't believe it's her, but there's absolutely no doubt who her momma is. Come on, promise I can handle it, just tell me."

I see Raven look to Tink, who is watching me and Sebastian. She gives a look to my ol' man then she nods to Raven. My sister looks at me, a very sad look on her face. Then she tears my world apart.

"Glory, we don't have her here because we aren't sure which compound she's at currently. Freak and I have been trying to go under the radar and search, but they have some good hackers. It's taking us time, but we will get it done."

Something Raven said hits me and I feel it immediately. My brain is playing catch-up, but did she say something about what compound she's at? The only time we use that word is in reference to that brotherhood of assholes. Oh my Lord, please don't tell me my daughter has been alive all this time and has been tortured, rape, and God knows what else all this time. I feel my head get hot and I'm having a hard time breathing. Feeling hands on me, I'm up and out of the room in less than five seconds.

"Bae, gotta breathe. I know this is breaking your heart, but you now know she's alive. We'll find her and bring her back here. You gotta believe that."

"Boo, I'm not gonna make it. Whatever is going on, if someone has harmed a hair on that girl's head, I will scalp whoever put hands or any other body part on my daughter. My God, Lilly is alive. What happened that day when Oscar took me? Where is Gino, and why did he allow that crazy as fuck brotherhood to have my daughter? I've tried to believe Gino wasn't a part of what went down, but now I'm not so sure. Son of a bitch, do you have any idea how she is? I mean Lilly, do you have anything that will tell me she's not only alive but okay?"

Then I feel the panic and anxiety rushing through my body, so I reach behind me for Sebastian, who grabs my hand, holding on to it tightly. When I shift and look at him, he is watching me like a hawk. Feeling suddenly hot, my head starts pounding and spinning. Feeling lightheaded, I scream over and over again.

"Lilly, Lilly, Lilly, Lilly, Lilly."

Right before I let the darkness take over and I pass out, my final thought is, *oh my God, my daughter is alive. And in my heart I can feel it, she's in danger.*

FIFTEEN
'TANK'
JAY

I see the minute Glory's brain shuts off, right before she starts to slip down after screaming her daughter's name in a voice I'll never forget. Pure tortured pain.

"Yoggie, grab her, don't let her hit the ground. Protect her head, for Christ's sake. Goddamn, this ain't the way it was supposed to go. Motherfucker, she's in shock. Move outta the way, assholes."

I stomp right to my brother Yoggie, who is carefully supporting Glory's weight. Everyone is trying to move around in this pissant of an office. Not my club, but fuck, someone's gotta take charge.

"Every motherfucker out, now. Enforcer, Yoggie, Maggie, Raven, and Freak stay. Yeah, you too, Zoey. No, we ain't got time to argue. Someone put a call into Dr. Cora, see where she's at. This is gonna fuck with Glory's head, might need something to calm her nerves down. Come on, Yoggie, get her over to that fuckin' miniature couch. Son of a bitch, she'll barely fit. For Christ's sake, why can't you women buy normal furniture for your offices?"

Even though her skulled face shows how worried she is, Zoey smirks my way. That's my girl, always able to get outta her head. Unlike my other girl, the president of this club. Maggie is running her hands through her hair, glaring at the computer screen.

"For Christ's sake, Raven, shut that shit down now. We don't need Glory to wake up and see that. She will immediately pass the hell out again. Not sure what to do, need a minute to think. Why would that brotherhood have Lilly? What's their purpose because they don't do anything without a goal in mind. I have no clue. Shit, this is gonna gut her. Why does this shit keep happening to our club? We're trying our best to make it a better world, I don't get it. Why does it seem like the entire universe is against each and every one of us."

Watching my daughter Maggie losing it, I do the only thing a father and fellow president can do. I piss her the fuck off.

"See, I told you years ago, Tink, that you weren't strong enough to handle this shit. Might want to, how do you women say, 'put your big girl panties on' or suck it up, however it makes sense to you. Your girl here is gonna need you with your head on straight so she can lean on you, for fuck's sake. Think you can do that, Prez?"

I watch and it takes maybe ten or fifteen seconds for that backbone to straighten up. Then those green eyes start flashing at me, right before she blows.

"What did you just say to me? Who the fuck do you think you are, talking to me like that in my own goddamn clubhouse? Get the hell out, old man, don't need your kind of help. I said, GET THE FUCK OUT NOW!"

The door slams open and there is my ol' lady, bags in her hands, eyes wide, as she looks from me to Maggie and back again. In that time span of looking at the door, when I glance back, Zoey is at Maggie's back, as always. And those icy-blue eyes, if they could kill, I'd be dead. Fuck, I can see why she freaks people out, never has she turned those on me. Before I can say a word, my wife steps up.

"I don't know what's going on here and I try to stay out of both of your clubs' bullshit, but after what I just heard I'm in. First, young lady, you will never speak to your father like that again. I don't give a rat's ass how old you are. And don't smirk, Jay, I'm sure you either said or did something to majorly piss Maggie off to lose it like that. And while you two children fight, who's taking care of Glory? Yoggie, I got her. Go get me some Jack Daniel's and a bowl with ice and a towel, please. No, don't ask, I know we can call someone. I'm trying to get a minute with my family so I can ream their asses in private. Freak, Raven, can I have the room?"

Watching my wife in full control has something growing and it ain't my adoration. This woman, even after all these years, can get my motor running. Though not the time or place as I have some cleanup to do. Diane is right, sometimes I am a bull in a china store.

"Baby girl, come here. No, now, Maggie. I just was trying to pull your head outta your ass. You've got this, like you've had everything that's been thrown at you. Come on, daughter of mine, you're one of the toughest women I know. I get you're worried about Glory, we all are, but we have to figure out what's going on and why. Then we can take care of business. 'Kay? You forgive your old man for being a total prick and not thinkin' before he runs his mouth off?"

Maggie looks up at me and it dawns on me how proud I am of her. Holding her tiny self with her Devil's Handmaidens MC kutte on, president patch on one side, it hits me hard in the gut how far she's come. I think to myself, *sometimes I don't give her and her club enough credit for all they do*. They all bust their asses to, as she says, make the world a better place while giving survivors a second chance to find a way to move forward and live.

Feeling her tiny arms wrap around my waist, I know I'm forgiven. Maggie has done this since she was a little girl. Never would she say the words '*I forgive you,*' she always had to show me. Grabbing hold of her with one mitt, the other goes up to her head, running over her hair. When a second pair of arms wrap around me from the back, I know it's Z. This is the way it's been since Maggie found her in that field so long ago. Zoey is a total badass unless you're one of us Rivers. Then she can turn to mush.

Yoggie comes running back in, a bottle of Jack under one arm while he has a bowl filled with ice and a hand towel. My ol' lady tells him to bring the bowl to her and

I see her wipe Glory's face. Yeah, that's my woman, always emotional. But strong as a bull too. She wraps the ice in the towel and places it on Glory's forehead. The minute it touches skin, Glory's eyes pop open and she immediately tries to look around, though Diane covers her eyes with the towel.

"Give it a minute, Glory. I need you to take a couple of deep breaths for me. Then if you feel like it, we'll get you up to a sitting position. So come on, breathe with me."

I stand with my two girls wrapped in my arms, thinking in that deep dark area in my head I'm done with these Thunder Cloud Knuckle Brotherhood jagoffs. Time to start a plan to rid the world of their existence. Might need some help or have to call in some markers, but I'll do whatever I have to, to protect my family.

We all wait as Diane murmurs to Glory, trying to put her at ease. My ol' lady is good at that, for sure. When Yoggie helps his ol' lady so she can sit up, no one says a word. Her eyes immediately go to the computer screen, but her face falls when she sees it dark. Can't imagine how she feels well, actually, I kinda can. When Hannah was taken it was like someone ripped my heart out of my chest. Feeling a heaviness in that area, I rub it while watching Diane. She's my one shining star and accomplishment, besides our girls.

It takes Glory about six minutes to pull herself together. In that time, I can hear the noise in the hallway getting louder and louder. Just goes to show how many people care about the VP of the Devil's Handmaidens.

She keeps glancing at the door then the blank computer screen. After about another five minutes, I give in.

"Glory, you ready? I'll get Raven and Freak back in here so they can share what they found out, only if you think you can handle it. No, don't do that, no one in this room is judging you. My God, woman, you just found out your little girl is alive and grown. That would fuck anyone's head up. So let that shit go. Need to find out all we can about your Lilly, then figure out a way to get her away from them. So am I calling in the troops or are we all gettin' drunk on Jack Daniel's?"

That brings a tiny smile to Glory's face, and I think to myself my work here is done. Glory looks to Yoggie and it's amazing to see them having a conversation with no words. That man is worth his weight in gold, and I'm thrilled to call him my brother. When they are done, Yoggie looks to me and gives me the signal, a chin lift, lettin' me know they are ready to move this show forward. *Great*, I think to myself as I lift off the chair and walk to the door, opening it. Fuck, the hallway is packed with bikers leaning against the walls and sitting their asses on the floor. Up front are Glory's sisters, who look beyond concerned. This room ain't big enough so I look to Maggie, who nods.

"Get your asses outta the hallway and back into the main room. Raven, can you bring a laptop or computer to share what you found?"

"Tank, I'm hooked up out there, can stream it through the projection television so, yeah, I'm good. Let me grab a few things and I'll be right out. Freak, want to grab your shit so we can share at the same time?"

My nerd of a brother nods but his eyes follow Raven's ass. Oh, fuck me NO. Brother, not that one, she'll eat ya up and spit ya out. Raven's a good woman but between her jokes and snipes she'd be a handful and not one I think Freak can handle. *Only time will tell*, I think to myself as I grab my ol' lady's hand and start to head to the main room to see what's gonna hit us next. Let's deal with this shit before one of my brothers stirs the pot for Christ's sake.

SIXTEEN
'YOGGIE'
SEBASTIAN

Never in my wildest dreams did I ever even consider that Nora's daughter was alive. As sad as that thought is, now I'm not so sure it's great news that she's alive. Yeah, what a shitty thought, but I always see the picture beyond what is first presented. Something ain't right, but I'm not involved in this as much as all the rest of Nora's crew. They have first-hand experience as they were there for her when she transferred out here after her husband and little girl were taken from her. She made the ultimate sacrifice for her family.

Hearing the door closing on Olivia's bedroom, I sit on the edge of the bed waiting for Nora. I can't imagine how hard this is for her, though I've had my own experiences when in the service that left me hollow. If I hadn't found the Intruders, I have no idea what would have become of me. I'm a team player and need to protect, so being the one who helps Enforcer keep Tank safe satisfies me to no end. Now with Nora and Olivia, my internal needs are being met by being allowed to keep them from the evils of the world. Though both females in this house have experienced the scum of the earth already.

Nora walks in and I can tell she's beyond exhausted. Emotionally drained. When she's right in front of me, I grab her hands, placing a kiss on the top of each. Then I stand, my hands cupping her head as I gently place a kiss on her perfect as fuck lips.

"Bae, get undressed and lie on the bed. No, don't ask any questions, just know I plan to take care of you. Trust me, Nora."

Then I let her go and walk to the door, locking it just in case Olivia tries to climb into our bed during the night. I don't mind but others might. She's not my daughter and she's approaching that age where she should be sleeping in her own bed. After the door is locked, I move to the bathroom, grabbing the basket I have sitting on the countertop.

I stop dead in my tracks when I enter the bedroom. Nora listened to me and is lying on the large towel I placed on top of the sheets, totally naked. The only things on her skin are her tattoos, which always draw my eyes to her. Her long hair is spread out on her pillow and her eyes are half-mast and sexy as fuck. Damn, this was gonna test my body's restraint, 'cause all I want to do is drop my clothes and crawl up her long sexy body and bury myself in her tight warmth all night long 'til we can't move and drop into a relaxed and utterly spent sleep.

Her eyes never leave mine as I approach her side of the bed, which is away from the door. As I keep telling her, I'll always have her back and protect her.

"Bae, turn over onto your belly. Come on, it'll be worth it, I promise, beautiful."

Watching her body shift and move has my dick starting to thicken up and lengthen so it is getting a bit uncomfortable. I undo the top button of my jeans but that's all I do. Tonight is not about me but about my Bae. I gaze at her long neck and smooth as silk back that narrows down to the two dimples right above her ass. And what an ass she has. It's heart-shaped with a bit of a bubble to it. Her legs are shapely and long. Not sure where to start, I put the basket on the bed, and kneel at the bottom of it.

With my hands now full of warmed oil, I start to massage the arches of her feet when I hear the sudden gasp followed by a low moan. Not exactly sensual but nonetheless it tells me I am in the right spot. Slowly I work first one then the other foot. After, I make my way up her legs and thighs. I don't quit or move on until I can feel her muscles actually relaxing and letting loose. By the time I warm more oil in my hands and place them on her ass, I hear the soft noises she makes when she's asleep. My Bae is letting it go for now. Now the rubbing and massaging is for me. I can never get enough of my hands on her body. Nora is not one of those women who tries to hide her body. No matter what, in our relationship it is equal, she takes and gives. And never hides or covers anything. I love that about her.

When I've worked my way up her back and finish her shoulders, I go down each arm, making sure the joints are also relaxed. After I'm done, I go back into the bathroom, this time shutting the door partially so I don't disturb her. I throw the towels I used in the laundry basket and put the oils and lotions away. Then I rip my T-shirt off and drop both my jeans and boxers.

I hit the shower making sure the water is on the cooler side so as not to bother the burned skin on my lower back and ass. Don't think anyone but Nora and Ironside know about my injuries. I've got other scars but those are the worst. I already told Nora that in the winter she'll have to help me keep the damaged skin moisturized or I can have issues. Been there done that, not going back.

I grab my body wash and quickly go over my body. Feeling the raised bumps on my thighs, I know how goddamn lucky I am to be alive as just about half of our team didn't come home, not because they were killed but because there was nothing left to bring home. My hand grabs my cock and I vigorously wash it and my balls before moving up to my chest. I can feel the weight of my cock as it gets harder, but I'm not going to beat myself off. No, it will be worth the wait to feel Nora tighten around me as I thrust into her. I love how she is open to just about anything, which makes our coming together not only interesting but sexually addicting too.

Finishing off with washing my hair, I rinse off, and grab a towel before shutting down the shower. I quickly dry off and do my usual deodorant, body spray, and then brush my teeth. Running a quick comb through my hair, I move to the bedroom, flipping the main light off, though we always leave the small one in the water closet on for Nora. She can't sleep in the dark thanks to that bastard Oscar. I go to my dresser, pull out a clean pair of boxer briefs, put them on, and head toward the bed.

Seeing Nora's face has my breath catch. Seems like my massage relaxed her enough to fall into a deep sleep. Her face is relaxed with none of the earlier tenseness and fear on it. Before I get into bed, I move back to the door and unlock it, and pull it open just a little bit for Olivia. Then I walk to Nora's side and reach under her pillow for her nightshirt. Then, somehow, I manage to get it on her before I pull the covers up and over her.

When I'm situated on my side, I pull my Bae to me, holding on to her closely as memories of a faraway place flash before my eyes. Nora told me about her time as a prisoner of someone, so I'm going to have to tell her about my time as a prisoner of war. It might help her to deal with the horrors she went through with Oscar. Even though our prisons were different, the torture, manipulation, and emotional damage is the same, no matter what or where you are. Not to mention when the someone or someones holding you are sadists. Nora's story tells me Oscar is a total sadist. If I ever have the pleasure of meeting him, before I rip his head off his shoulders, he will get a small sampling of how a real sadist inflicts pain. I'm not a sadist but the motherfuckers who held me for fifteen months were, so I've been instructed by the best.

Not wanting to fight those nightmares before I try to sleep, I run my hands up and down Nora's side, trying to imagine our lives a year, two years, and even five years from now. And I come to the same conclusion, if we don't rescue Lilly there won't be a future for any of us. I'm glad that Freak and Raven are on it and are doing everything within their nerd powers to give us a complete picture of Nora's daughter's situation.

Feeling Nora shift, I lie here hoping my thoughts aren't what's breaking her sleep. She needs a good night's sleep, so that's what she'll get, if I have to stay awake all night and chase her demons away. I meant it when I told her that this is it for me. I'll always protect her. Now that includes Olivia and if or when Lilly gets here, she'll also have my protection. Nothing will ever hurt these three females ever again if I have any say-so.

My eyes are starting to droop so I close them, trying to relax my body section by section. Right before I start to drift, I hear it softly whispered. I'm not sure if she's awake or asleep, but her words bring a smile to my lips right before I fall asleep.

"Thanks, Sebastian, for actually being a good guy and helping to hold me up. I'll never be able to repay you, but I'll damn sure try. Thanks, Boo. Night."

SEVENTEEN
'TINK'
MAGGIE\GOLDILOCKS

Sitting in my downstairs family room, leaning up against Noodles, I watch as Zoey takes another two pieces of pizza while Panther just watches her, shaking his head. Sometimes I wonder about those two. My bestie seems to be able to eat just about anyone under the table. Well, except the one on the other side of her, reaching for three more pieces of pizza and two mozzarella sticks. Avalanche and Zoey have a constant food battle going on. I've come to the conclusion they are both totally insane. My man gives my shoulder a squeeze, letting me know he's about to drop a bomb.

"All right, let's get the huge elephant out in the open. What the hell are we gonna do about Glory's shit? I know you all talked it to death with your dad, Sweet Pea, but was a plan put in place? I spoke to Ollie and he said that whatever you need, just let him know. And he means anything, you all know he has connections all over now since the Blue Sky Sanctuary is on the map.

He's getting huge brownie points for all he's doing for our ex-military brothers and sisters. Just say the word, though I know you want to handle it yourselves. Sometimes it's not considered a weakness but a strength to ask for help. Just sayin'."

Watching everyone's faces, I know this is going to turn into a long discussion and, to be honest, I'm beyond exhausted. Haven't been feeling myself the last couple of days. Not sure if I'm catching something, as I know that Vixen's kids were sick last week, so it's just a matter of time before everyone in the club gets it. Also, the Wooden Spirits Bar and Grill is packed every night and Peanut told me just yesterday at the clubhouse that it's a petri dish of germs. She asked if they could close a little early on Sunday so a bunch of the sisters could do a deep clean. I told her it's fine, as long as a sign is posted on the doors of the bar and grill. She's the only person I know who gets so excited to clean the restaurant and bar. *Can I say OCD*, I think to myself.

I look over to Zoey, who's starting to look a bit off color. Oh shit, she better not puke like the last time when she went up against Avalanche, betting who could eat the most hot dogs. I don't think she's eaten one since. Knowing I'm going to have to save her, I give Noodles an elbow, then stare at him, and then the pizza. He nods, leaning over and grabbing the last four pieces, making a show of being starved, when I know after the five or six pieces he ate already, he's probably full. But my ol' man will do anything I ask.

"As Noodles said, I know that usually this is all

handled by the Devil's Handmaidens club, but know that my men are at your disposal for whatever you need. Tomorrow, Chicago and Dallas have to go a few towns over to pick up a horse, but outside of that we'll all be at the ranch. And that guy over there is gonna need to work off all that pizza he is stuffing down his face. Now, not sure about each of you, but Nizhoni and I had a rough night last night with our wolf dogs, so think we're going to call it a night.

"Thanks, Tink, for putting both myself and Avalanche up again. That drive to the ranch at this time of night can be treacherous, especially since my woman will want to ride her beast of a bike. Last time we did that, I almost drove off the road when we took a turn too fast and there was a herd of deer on the road. Zoey was able to stop, but not before her front tire bumped one of the huge beasts. Thought we were going to have to shoot him but he snorted loudly then slowly walked off into the woods. So we all agree, if it's too late we stay, if that's all right with you and Noodles."

Zoey is getting greener by the minute so I nod quickly.

"Panther, you guys are always welcome. Go on up to bed, we'll clean up. I know how early you both, no I mean all three of you, get up on that ranch of yours. Are your guys going to take care of the two howlers tonight?"

"Yeah, since Chicago and Dallas have to leave so early, they are spending the night at the ranch. Both Ma'iitsoh *(wolf)* and Zhį́'ii *(raven)* love the guys, so it'll be okay. Personally, I hate leaving them but nothing we can do about it. This takes precedence. A sister of Zoey's is like a sister of ours."

Avalanche, who's been quiet up 'til this moment, bumps shoulders with my bestie, a huge grin on his face.

"Little skull anii', might want to get a move on *'going to bed'* before you make a total fool outta yourself. Once again I win, even though you'll never admit it. Now get a movin', I'll see ya in the morning. Panther, go, I'll put a call out to George so they know what to do with the beasts. Sleep tight, don't let the bugs bite."

Zoey leaps up, hand to her mouth, running up the stairs as I hear Avalanche roaring with laughter. So much so, he has to grab a napkin as he chokes on his last piece of pizza. Panther starts beating him on the back as he lifts his hands high in the air. We watch as his face goes red and gets redder by the minute. Not sure if he is laughing or choking, I just stare but Noodles is up in a second, pulling him up, and wrapping his arms around his waist.

When I realize he's trying to do the Heimlich, Panther is holding his best friend still as he's trying to struggle while choking. On the fourth or fifth thrust from Noodles, a huge piece of pizza comes flying out of Avalanche's mouth just as Zoey comes back down the stairs, wiping her mouth. She sees what's going on and freezes on the stairs, mouth wide open. Noodles lets Avalanche go while Panther grabs him by the waist, holding his weight up. Avalanche's color is off and his eyes are tearing. He looks at Noodles for a long minute.

"Brother, I owe you. Goddamn, felt it get stuck but thought a cough or two and it'd be good. Zoey, we need to quit this childish shit 'cause, eventually, your throat is gonna be damaged from all your puking or I'm gonna choke to death. What the fuck is wrong with us? Glory is going through hell and we are acting like two little kids. Let's make a pact that we quit with the stupid shit and just realize we like each other, and that's okay."

She comes down the stairs and walks right to Avalanche, putting her arms around his waist.

"Thank God, Big Bird, I'm getting sick of throwing up my food all the time. Now, are you okay, or do we need Dr. Cora to make a house call?"

He shakes his head again, looking Noodles's way.

"Nope, that one saved my life. And in our culture when you save a life the one you saved is indebted to you for their entire life. So, Noodles, whatever you need, all you have to do is reach out and I'll be there. That's a promise. Tomorrow, what I'm gonna do when you two head back to the ranch is I'll take a ride to where that old compound was for the Thunder Cloud Knuckle Brotherhood. Something tells me they are hiding Glory's daughter Lilly somewhere close. Maybe I'll go look at the De Luca mansion too. Or what's left of it. They aren't gonna build from scratch, but with their contacts I could see them getting help from high places."

Noodles looks to me then to Avalanche, and I know what he's going to say before it comes out of his mouth.

"Avalanche, plan on Phantom and me joining you. Don't want you to go off half-cocked. And if you do see something, might get dangerous for you by yourself. And no, I'm not saying you can't handle yourself, but these assholes are lethal. So, you good with us tagging along?"

"Yeah, Noodles, sounds good. I'll give ya a call when I'm getting ready. You gonna call Phantom or do you want me to?"

As the two men figure out the hows and whens, I give Zoey a look and she gives me a half-ass grin. Yeah, she's glad this is over. I'm ready to fall over so I get up, grabbing my bestie's hand, and together we walk up the stairs so we can take a minute to ourselves. We go into the kitchen and each grab a bottle of water. No words are needed as we gulp down our water.

"You going to be okay, Zoey?'

"Yeah, Goldilocks, just glad I don't have to keep trying to keep up with Big Bird. We should call him Godzilla the way he eats, for God's sake. I've gained twelve pounds since this competition started. Gotta start working out harder and get this weight off before I'm not able to fit into my clothes."

I look at her and she doesn't look like she's put on a pound. And as far as working out, besides Rebel, I don't know anyone else who works out more than Shadow. Though I'll let her think she's got to get off her ass, it might keep her off of mine. Then she drops her bomb.

"So get ready, Goldilocks, you need to get up an hour early so we can hit the gym together. No, not gonna listen to your excuses, you been getting soft since

Noodles came into your life. I'm gonna need to toughen you up, ya know, being president and all."

For a quick second I give her a shocked face then we both start to crack up. That is what the guys walk into, us laughing like idiots.

EIGHTEEN
'YOGGIE'
SEBASTIAN

My God, I've never had a dream like this. I can feel my Bae's body suck me into the most intense heat I've ever felt, and that's saying a lot being a man my age. I've had my number of women, not bragging, but shit I was in the military and now I'm a member of a one-percent motorcycle club.

When Nora lifts her body up, almost all the way off of me, then slams back down I can't hold the moan that comes outta my mouth.

I've got no problem giving up power to this woman. No matter if I'm being dominant or submissive, the end is always good for both of us. Nora generally is the submissive one, probably because of all of her responsibilities as VP. But now she's got her dominant side going and I'm totally digging it. When she pulls my hands above my head, wrapping my fingers around the headboard, I do exactly what she wants. Then she starts to kiss her way down my neck to my chest. When her mouth sucks one of my nipples in, I take in a deep breath right before she bites down. Not too hard but also not too soft. My cock feels like it's about to burst, but I let her continue with that magical mouth of hers. Lower and lower she goes licking, sucking, and nibbling. When she gets to my belly button, her hands come into play, caressing my nuts, first one then the other.

By the time she gets me in her mouth I am just about ready to explode. Not wanting her to think I assume how this will end, I finally speak.

"Bae, I'm so close, not gonna last."

She nods then takes me deep. By the time she does it for the third time I feel the familiar tingles running up and down my entire body, while the muscles in my back and ass tense up. When my balls pull up into my body, I'm lost to the sensations. I curl my toes into the comforter as Nora moans, taking me deep. That's when I explode and actually lose time.

When I can finally catch my breath, and once again Nora is lying on top of me, her head right under my chin, I lean down and place a kiss on the top of her head.

"What was that for, Nora? My God, woman, you're gonna kill me one of these days, though I'm not complaining at all. Best way to go."

She giggles and that right there tells me she's okay, though her world cracked open yet again. She hung on to Olivia tonight and stayed in her bedroom long after the little girl was asleep. By the time she came to our room, I'd showered and was reading my book. I could tell she was exhausted. When she crawled into bed, she snuggled close, telling me she needed comforting, so I pulled her close, rubbing my hand slowly up and down her back until she fell asleep, which I followed her not too long after.

"Bae, how are you really doing? I can't even imagine what's going on in your head but I'll be around, just in case. Now get that fine ass of yours up here, I've got a taste only you can satisfy."

Again, she giggles as she crawls up my body and then she is the one holding on to the headboard.

* * *

Not sure what woke me up, but I carefully get out of bed and pull on my sweats. Looking down at Nora, I smile then walk to the door, opening it and starting down the hallway when I hear a faint whining sound. Not sure what it is, I open Olivia's door to see she's curled up in a ball under her covers, holding on to her polar bear, Ivory.

As I go to shut her door, the whining starts again but it's closer this time. Something in the back of my mind is triggered, and before I know it, I'm walking toward the front door. Reaching in the hallway closet, I open the gun safe built into the wall. Nora said it's something all the houses, cabins, and main house have. Grabbing my Glock and two clips that I put in my pocket, I lock the safe back up, and go to the front door, opening it.

Bright lights hit me directly in the eyes, blinding me for a second. I stumble my way out the front door, and it hits me where I've heard this sound before was when I was in the service, it is a motherfucking drone. They have a unique whine, especially when they are low to the ground. When my eyes have adjusted, I look up and there are three drones making circles around our house. What the fuck? If Raven thinks this is funny, it's not. Just as I go to move, one of the drones comes down really low and I swear to Christ it's following my every move. The feeling going down my spine warns me as the drone dives right toward me. Hitting the porch, I land behind the storage bench. Thank God because I could have sworn I heard bullets.

Son of a bitch, that thing is shooting at me. I lean to the left, aiming my gun, firing through my entire clip. Thank God, one winged it as I see sparks before it does a few circles and tries to take off after the other two, hightailing it out of here. Then I hear the noise and it's getting louder and louder, just as the front door flies open and Nora is standing there with a Steyr AUG SA USA rifle in her hands. Well, fuck me, where the hell did she have that hidden? Just when I'm about to ask her, the noise is deafening as bike after bike come flying up the road to our house. Behind the bikes are a few pickup trucks.

Nora lets the gun down, holding it in one hand while lifting the other high up in the air, shaking it back and forth. Not sure what she's doing, but not my circus, not my monkey as the old saying goes. I walk up next to Nora, grabbing her Steyr, taking a close look at it. She looks at me, shaking her head.

"Just like a guy, no matter what is going on they have to check out the new gun. What's going on, Sebastian?"

I just shake my head as one by one Devil's Handmaidens sisters come up to us, and it hits me that every one of the women here were probably up at the main house. Then I see Raven making her way up to us. She grabs Nora, pulling her in closely, hugging her tightly.

"Holy fuck, Glory, all I did was go to the bathroom and splash water on my face. Swear to Christ, not even gone for five minutes. Then my alarms started going off and when I saw those motherfuckers in the sky, I hit the warning on everyone's phones. All I could think back on is all the drama when Vixen's shit was going down. Remember when Slick showed up in the bomb vest and then the drone showed up. Sister, I'm sorry, never going to piss again, swear to you."

That brings a snort then a laugh from Nora as she holds on tightly to the younger woman. Just looking at Raven, you can tell she's freaked out. When I look around the two women, I see Squirt with Olivia in her arms, trying to calm her down. When everyone sees the young girl, they try to hide or cover their weapons up. Olivia smiles hugely.

"Oh no, did I miss the action? Dang it, Squirt, how could I sleep during a mission? Does that mean I have to give my kutte back? I swear, I'll never sleep again. You can depend on me, sisters."

That, on top of Raven's promise never to urinate

again, has everyone grinning and/or smiling. That's when I hear Nora whispering to Raven, who is now standing next to her.

"Raven, sister, I can't thank you enough. Once again you have my back. No, don't go there, if you weren't still up and watching the screens, only God knows what would have happened. So knock it off. Did you see anything else or did you leave the computers recording as you came and played hero again?"

With that, Nora shoulder bumps Raven again and again until she grins, which has my ol' lady grinning back. Then a whistle sounds and we all look at Shadow.

"All right, nothing more can be done tonight. I want two sisters here until the morning. Also, Avalanche has volunteered to stay and keep watch so the three of you can stay in his truck. Squirt, you and Heartbreaker stay, put your bikes in the pole barn. Avalanche, park your truck under the carport over there. Everyone else back to the main house or wherever the fuck you came from. Cynthia, go on, you and the kids get back to the bunkhouse. Tell the bunch there that everything is okay. Tink and I will talk to them in the morning. Yeah, thanks, Cynthia."

I'm shocked as I didn't even notice Cynthia and her kids were out of the bunkhouse. When I turn that's when I notice that Cynthia, the timid ex-bank manager, with a rifle in her arms. One kid had a can of Mace and the other a Taser. Well, fuck me, guess they've been trained by the Devil's Handmaidens sisters.

Everyone starts to move along, though Nora hangs

on to Raven just as Squirt brings Olivia over to us. As soon as she puts her down, Olivia has her arms up to Nora, who picks her up. Then my ol' lady leans into her sister.

"Raven, go back to the main house and get some sleep. No, don't argue with me, listen up. Brenna, I can't thank you enough but you're burning the candle at both ends, and you're going to fuck yourself up. Please go get some sleep. I'll tell Tink to have Dani or Dotty go sit in your office up at the main house and watch your computers. They've watched them for you before, so the twins know what to look for. You need to take care of yourself or you'll be no good to the club."

Raven looks at Nora then slowly nods. When she goes to turn, Squirt walks up to her, grabbing her hand, and walking down with her toward her bike. I can hear whispering and look to see Nora and Olivia's heads together. Then I hear the little girl and what she says has me wanting to find the bastards and tear them apart with my own hands.

"Nora, was those the flying things in the sky? Those mean men had those at that place you found me at. They sometimes would make some of the other girls stand in the big field and they would shoot at them. One time they hit Sasha in the foot and then another time the rocks hit Kathy in the face. Juice got mad at them but they told him to shut his, they used a bad word, mouth. And he did. I think he was scared of them, which was good because we was scared of him and them."

Nora meets my eyes over Olivia, and I know she

feels exactly like I do. Those motherfuckers need to pay for all the agony they've caused. Got to talk to Tank and Enforcer tomorrow. We need to step up our efforts to rid the world of the Thunder Cloud Knuckle Brotherhood for good, no matter what it takes.

NINETEEN
'DUTCHESS'
SISSY

Damn, I hate these long as shit nights when I'm stuck here at our trucking company, but someone's got to fix the damn rigs when they go down. And since I'm one of the mechanics, I volunteered because what else do I have to do. Go back to my little cabin on Tink's ranch and eat a frozen dinner, while I dive into my Kindle on to the next book on my TBR list? Seems like now I've much more time on my hands since my sisters in the Devil's Handmaidens are falling fast. I mean, I'm happy for them but, damn, so far four have found their men and it looks like Glory is quickly catching up to them with Yoggie.

Gotta say, our VP has excellent taste. When he first started to prospect with Tank's club I couldn't take my eyes off of him, as he looks more like a male model than a biker. And he's polite and always there to lend a hand. Even though he's hot as can be, Yoggie never acts like an asshole or dick like some of the men in our small community. With the growing number of bastards hanging with the Thunder Cloud Knuckle Brotherhood, my prospects of finding a 'man' are quickly going down the toilet.

As I work on the transmission of this beast, I've already changed a valve and the pump, so wiping my hands, I take a quick minute to grab a bottle of water and analyze what's left that could be broken. Taking a huge gulp, I hear something almost like an animal is scratching at the big door we pull the tractors in for service. Moving to the small desk in the corner, I pull up the camera and am totally shocked because all I see is black. What the ever-lovin' fuck is going on? Then I hear that same noise but louder now.

Very carefully and quietly I walk to the other side of the garage, where we have windows that folks can't see in but we can see out. What I see sends a shiver down my spine. There are at least four or five, I'm assuming men, in ski masks and dark clothing messing around out there. Two are throwing down garbage by the doors, while one other is grabbing whatever sticks and shit they can get their hands on. The last two have some kind of box or something they are messing with. Oh damn, this ain't good.

Reaching in my pocket, I pull my cell out and send the SOS text not one of my Devil's Handmaidens sisters ever wants to type or receive. It means serious trouble, need help now. As I go to put my phone back in my pocket, all of a sudden, an extremely loud alarm starts going off as lights on the outside start blinking on and off. As I watch in total shock, the five idiots seem to panic and run back to a large black vehicle parked on the inside of the gate that is now halfway closed.

As they all jump into the vehicle, I hear a faint sound like someone's horn. Not paying attention, I'm trying to get as much information on these scumbags so we can try and figure out who the hell they are and what they are doing here. Then, as they try to fit between the fence and the closing gate, I see the Wooden Spirits Bar and Grill catering van come wheeling down the driveway. Not sure who's driving but these guys have a purpose, which is to get the fuck outta Dodge.

I squeeze my eyes closed for a quick second because not sure I want to see how these two vehicles come together. Well, it's not to the benefit of the five assholes, that's for sure. As they try to manipulate their humongous SUV past the gate, which is now jammed into the side of their vehicle, the catering van's side window goes down as one of our Steyr AUG SA USA rifles comes out, pointing at the large vehicle. When whomever starts firing, first goes the tires on that side then a round goes through the back windows by the third-row seating. As our club van rolls by slowly, someone has some kind of a can and now that there is an opening, they toss it in and take off like bats outta hell.

Immediately smoke starts to fill up that part of the vehicle, and it's not a minute or so before the doors open and the two masked assholes in the front come rolling out onto the concrete, hands up, guns dropped on the ground. The two in the second row also open their doors but they come out fighting, which is beyond stupid because by now we've got people rolling in left and right.

With my attention on what's happening outside, I don't feel it until I hear boots on the concrete. Turning, I see Peanut and Wildcat making their way to me. When they see me, they smirk just for a second before they are stoic again. More gunfire is happening out front but they both walk right up to me. Wildcat grabs me, looking me up and down.

"Sister, goddamn, ya okay? Thank God, Raven put that security on all of our phones. We're fucking lucky that she knows her shit. I keep saying that to the powers that be too. Now whatcha know, Duchess? Got anything to share or we gonna wait for Shadow to get here, probably with Rebel? Together I'm sure they'll be able to pull out what they were doing here, and why they have a bomb in a box with a timer that detonates when a call comes in. Hope Vixen keeps her pregnant ass home, she's starting to really get on my last nerve with all of her all-day sickness. Last time we had that issue at the grill with the mice, she not only wanted us to catch them but bring them back to the ranch and give them a home. Ya know how good that went with Shadow and Tink. The poison worked really fast and, shit, I swear to Christ she cried the whole next day, calling our sisters 'baby mice killers.' That had Shadow first snorting then laughing so hard she had to run before she pissed her pants. And that pissed off our enforcer so she came back with huge attitude.

"I even suggested to Tink that maybe she find something for Vixen to do that's not related to our missions for the time being. We will see if it goes anywhere."

Turning when I hear more vehicles, I look to see Sheriff George getting out of his squad car, while Rebel and Kitty are pulling the couple of assholes still in the huge SUV out by whatever they can grab. The first two are now in cuffs and are being escorted to a sheriff's squad. Chaos that's what it is again at one of our businesses.

I feel her before I even see her skull face. Shadow comes right through the large door someone opened and stomps right to me, grabbing me by the arms.

"You okay, kid? Did good, kept your head clear. I'll get what we need quickly from them. Heat up the torch, will ya, Duchess? Wildcat grab some rope and zip ties. Gonna go talk to my dad real fast, be right back." She turns and moves like lightning to her father, Sheriff George. When he sees her, a small smile appears on his face until she starts talking. He's shaking his head at first, but then his arms are in the air as he gets riled up. I'm sure Shadow is demanding this go her way but, unfortunately, the sheriff has to abide by the law. Well, most of the time.

As their words become heated, another pickup makes its way to the shop. When it's close enough, I can see it's Noodles and Tink. He stops right by the open overhead door, as our prez jumps down from the running boards. She looks around then her eyes stop on the five men on the ground before she looks and finds me. Then she's on the move, coming my way.

"Duchess, you good, sister? What the hell happened? I almost crapped myself when the alarm went off on my phone. Jesus Christ, had no clue what it was until Noodles told me. So what do we know? Do we know what their intentions were? Thought I heard someone on the two-ways say a bomb was found. Come on, give it to me, so I can figure out how to move forward with this and try not to involve any innocents, if possible. This town has had enough shit to last a decade, for sure. The only thing we got going for us right now is that it's the middle of the night. Hey, Duchess, why were you here alone, sister? Thought we all agreed to do things in twos until some of this shit died down. It could have gone really shitty real fast, remember that. I'm not trying to be a bossy bitch, just don't want anything to happen to any of us because of that brotherhood. I'm sure they'd gang rape one of us without thinking twice. Now, let's get this cleaned up so Zoey can do her thing and we can finally get some answers."

I watch as Tink approaches the sheriff, who's speaking to Noodles. She seems so tiny and fragile, but I've seen my prez bring down men bigger than Noodles and even Avalanche. We all say she's tiny and mighty.

I shake my head and start out to see what's going on and where we go from here. One thing for sure, it's not getting any easier, that's for damn sure. And now the job I was almost done with will go to the back burner and we'll be down one tractor tomorrow, which will throw everything off. Gonna have to put a call out to Pussy so he can switch shit around since he's been helping out in dispatch now that his ol' lady just had their second—no, I think third kid. They fuck like rabbits, though I smile to myself, their children are adorable. Two girls and the last is a little boy.

With that thought I reach for my cell so I can fill him in, then do whatever needs to be done. Seems like the assholes did some damage around the yard and to some of our trucks. Gonna be another long night. Our club is getting worn out with all of this bullshit, and we're no closer to finding Glory's kid or bringing down the brotherhood. Something's gonna have to switch up 'cause not sure how much longer we can do this. Especially if we find a human trafficking circuit that needs to be broken up. *Too much on our plates, as usual*, I think right when Pussy picks up and I start to explain the situation.

TWENTY
'SHADOW'
ZOEY

That the sounds of these men in agony calms my nerves, says a lot about how I've dealt with my life. I'm in the downstairs of the trucking company, in the last bay. I have Rebel, Wildcat, Avalanche, and Panther helping me. There's five of us working on five of the Thunder Cloud Knuckle Brotherhood assholes. I made sure Rebel and Wildcat had two of the more passive jerks since they are learning from me. Just in case, you never know what will happen, and our club needs at least one insane enforcer and so far, they both are holding their own.

Avalanche has one of the biggest jagoffs I've seen in this kind of situation. Though Big Bird has surprised me tonight with his way of getting information from this big mouth racist prick. Since we are in our garage and not at my wet room we have to improvise and, man, does he ever. His prisoner is hanging by chains from the main level into the bottom bay. His toes are lying on the ground and at the moment Avalanche is pulling the skin off of his feet that he burned with a torch. At this point the asshole is begging to tell us whatever we want. So much so that Avalanche stuffed a rag in his mouth.

Panther works another way. He plays mind games with his prisoner. The man was blindfolded immediately so he has no idea what's going on. He hears the moans and screams of his friends so he naturally assumes he will be getting the same treatment. Panther, though, doesn't do that. By the time he goes to put his hands on the man, his mind has been so manipulated and fucked up he's screaming like a banshee just from Panther cracking or pinching him.

It's been a few hours and we've gotten a few things out of them but, let's face it, these are the bottom feeders. The ones with all the power aren't sharing their plans with these guys. In all reality, they are sent and considered collateral damage. So, I ask the question I need answers too.

"Motherfucker, were is Lilly and don't act like you don't know who she is to us. If you work with us, I'll make sure you die quick and painless. Otherwise, by the time I'm done with you you'll be begging everyone you've ever known to put you out of your misery and pain. So, let's try this again, where is Lilly being kept?"

"Even if I knew and told you, it won't help you get her outta there. She'll never leave, they have her right where they want her."

After a few planned strikes on his already bruised body, I pull my hunting knife out and start to make crisscross cuts on his chest. Not too deep, but deep enough so he feels it. And by the way he's flinching and trying to pull back when I get close, it tells me his nerves are firing on all the right circuits. Getting a bit more zealous, I cut through some muscle which has him howling. Now we're getting somewhere.

"Why do you think Lilly wouldn't leave if we were to go and rescue her? Probably would be the best day of her life getting away from your psycho club."

"Well, your demented bitch Lilly has been trained from when she was a young girl, and she knows what happens if she disobeys by the way she's been taught. Now, the reason she won't ever leave—well not for the next ten to twelve years—is because if she walks away Lilly will never see her child again."

The rage takes over immediately when what he says registers in my head. Not sure how, but the next thing I remember is Panther screaming at me in Navajo while at the same time Avalanche walks up to the jagoff. I am literally chopping into him with my Bowie. He grabs the knife out of my hand and slits the guy's throat. Seeing the blood squirt all over, it dawns on me that I feel like I'm watching from above and not in my own body. How in the fuck am I supposed to tell my friend and sister, Glory, that the daughter who was taken away from her years ago is now a mother herself? And shit, Lilly has to be no older than Squirt's age, which I believe Hannah is almost twenty. So that means Lilly's about eighteen-ish. Got to find out how old her child is. I walk to the next prick, who's watching me with huge eyes that are leaking wet. Fuck you, asshole, you'll be meeting the devil tonight for sure.

"One question and then you won't suffer any longer or else, I swear to God, I'll pull you apart layer by layer. When you've been skinned, I'll gut you and wrap your guts around your neck, using them to strangle you. Now I want the truth. How old is Lilly's child, and is it a boy or girl?"

He swallows nervously, looking at the other guys in the room. At this point it's everyone for themselves. He looks me straight into my dead icy-blue eyes.

"I don't know for sure, not good at guessin' but I'm think she's between like nine, ten or eleven years old. I've never even seen the girl, but from what I've been told she's as gorgeous as her momma. But that's hearsay."

I can see and smell his fear but I gave him my word, so I reach to the table, pulling my Sig, and put a bullet right between his eyes. All of a sudden, the exhaustion takes over and I scream for Rebel and Wildcat to move, and I shoot the remaining three men. Enough is enough. We found out all we would have, so now got to figure out how to break the news to Glory.

"Motherfucker. How the fuck am I going to be able to tell Glory that her baby was raped and had a baby when she wasn't even a teenager? I want to jump in the truck, or better yet, on my bike and find each and every one of those in the brotherhood and put them to ground. Panther, I can't deal with this, it's going to literally obliterate our VP's heart and soul. And she's finally moving on and trying to live. And they say there's a God, then why does he do shit like this to people who've suffered enough?"

Feeling my emotions start to bubble over, I'm shocked when Avalanche tells my two sisters to go upstairs and find some cleaning supplies so they can start cleaning the place up. After, he walks directly to me, pulling me into him. Then he shocks the shit out of me.

"Zoey, you'll tell her quickly, like pulling off a Band-Aid. Then you and the rest of your Devil's Handmaidens sisters will be there for her to hold her up. I've seen it time and time again, so take a breath, for Christ's sake. You've got this, little skull anii'. I have all the faith in you, so don't start second-guessing yourself. Now let me go upstairs, give you two a minute or two alone. Don't make me regret this because if I come down and you two are fucking around, I'll be pissed. Mainly because I don't have that option. Be back in a few."

Watching him go, it dawns on me I've not been calling him Big Bird. Ever since he honestly told me he hated it; I've been trying to continue to build our relationship because he's Panther's best friend and brother. I can't let it go now though.

"Hey, Big Bird. No matter what I say, know this now, I'll always have your back and we will find you that someone you can share shit with or even fuck around with. Now get, brother."

I watch his shoulders lift then settle back down before he turns my way. The look in his eyes tells me everything I need to know. Then he gifts me with his gorgeous smile, and I wonder why he's still single. Not the time or place, so going to put that on the back burner. We got enough shit right in front of us to deal with. Then when I'm done, no matter what time, I'll get my ass over to Glory's and find a way to tell her what we found out tonight. Then we figure a way to get both Lilly and her little girl out of whatever compound she's in.

Feeling arms pulling me against his hard body, I relax as soon as Panther's body presses into me. He always knows how to bring me down and out of my own insane and fucked-up mind. My thoughts are running crazy, thinking what poor Lilly went through as a child, it makes me want to kill whoever did that to her with my bare hands.

"Zoey, let it go. She will be okay. Look at all you've gone through and see where you are at now. Life is a circle and we don't control how it spins and moves throughout our lives. All we can do is our best with what we are given. Now if we all work together, we can get this cleaned up pretty quickly. What are we doing with their bodies, Nizhoni?"

As I think about it, I hear Avalanche making a racket on his way back down, just to let us know they were on their way. Looking at the carnage before me, I go through our options then turn to my ol' man.

"Let's make it easy. Instead of burying them with lye, tell one of the girls to go pull in that beater out back.

We'll throw them in there and burn it. Should take care of our problem, don't you think, Panther?"

He squeezes me tightly then nods in agreement. So much for an early night. Because after this, I'm putting a call out to Goldilocks to meet me at Glory's. One of the few times I need someone there with me to give this type of news. And I know it's going to kill my best friend as this is how she conceived Hannah so many years ago. Fuck, this shit has to stop happening. What is our goddamn world coming to?

TWENTY-ONE
'TINK'
MAGGIE\GOLDILOCKS

Hearing my cell ringing, I immediately knock Noodles's arm off of me and jump out of bed. Seeing Zoey's number, I start to freak out. Not sure I can handle much more; my hormones are all over the place.

"Zoey, everything okay?"

"Goldilocks, not even close. If I didn't have to tell you this, believe me I wouldn't, but gonna need you at Glory's as soon as you can get there. We got the motherfuckers to talk after a bit of persuasion. We've been told Lilly is in fact at one of the compounds, though none of these jackasses know which one. What they did have knowledge of is that even if we were to find her and try to take her away, she won't go."

"Why not? Is it because her dad is there too? Something has to be holding her there, right? Is she hooked up with one of those sick bastards, or does she have something like Stockholm syndrome, not realizing that those are not her protectors but abusers? Well, just spit it out, Zoey, what the hell is it you're so afraid to tell me?"

The silence is almost deafening. This must be even worse than I thought would come out of her questioning them tonight. As I wait, I look to see Noodles getting dressed, and for a quick second I think what a waste to cover all that manliness up. He looks my way and by the smirk on his face it's like he's in my head. I just give him a tiny grin.

"Goldilocks, the smart one of the bunch realized he was dead, no matter what, so he informed us that the reason Lilly won't leave is because if she does, she will never see her child again. He even implied that they might even go as far as killing the child to show the other women what would happen if they thought it was okay."

I didn't hear a word after she said Lilly and child. My God, she was a baby when Glory left. When did the Thunder Cloud Knuckle Brotherhood get ahold of her? And at what age did someone rape her little girl body? I can feel the shakes start just as the phone falls out of my hand onto the floor. Then my legs give out and I'm on my knees, looking at the phone, hearing my bestie screaming at the top of her lungs.

Within seconds Noodles is at my side, on his knees, pulling me close and holding on tightly to me. The shakes keep getting worse and my mind flashes back to when I was in my dad's clubhouse and I was drugged and raped. As I've always said, the only good thing that came from that horrific night is Hannah.

"Sweet Pea, talk to me. What's going on? Are you okay? Maggie, my God, did someone get hurt from the club? Is it your dad or mom? Fuck this."

Then he grabs my phone, screaming into it for, I'm guessing, Zoey to shut the fuck up and listen. Then he chews her ass out, never taking a breath as he gives her an ass beating. Then as quick as he started, he stops. His eyes are on me as he listens to what Zoey is telling him. I watch his face turn a pasty white and his mouth get tight. He takes a deep breath then tells my bestie he'll call her back in a minute.

When he disconnects the phone, he literally throws it on the floor then stands, walks over to the wall, and starts punching it not once or twice, but three times. Then his head hits the wall as his hands form fists at his side. I've never seen him like this. He's usually calm and steady so I'm starting to freak out. When he turns looking at me, his face guts me. I quickly get to my feet, rushing to him. My arms go around his waist as he pulls me in close.

We stay like this for a minute or two then he gently pushes me away.

"Sweet Pea, I don't even know what to say to make this better. It's so fucking bad and it's going to get worse. Glory has been beating herself up all these years. What the hell, do you think she's going to be able to handle it when she gets this information about the daughter she thought might have been in hiding with her father or, worst-case scenario, dead. Now the good news is Lilly is alive but, my God, what shape is she going to be in? And that poor child who was conceived out of hate and brutality. We need to end that bunch of motherfuckers, Maggie. Now we need to get dressed and get over to Glory and Yoggie's before Shadow does. And while you're getting dressed, gonna put a call out to Raven to alert every Devil's Handmaidens sister to meet at Glory's. She'll need all the support she can get, that's for sure. And know, Sweet Pea, I'm right at your side and here for you, no matter what."

Feeling the tears running down my face, I lean into Noodles as he hugs me tightly.

"Noodles, I know exactly what that little girl not only went through but also the emotional roller coaster with your feelings toward that baby. So yeah, you're right, Glory is going to need each and every one of us there to support her. I'm going to get dressed. Thanks soldier boy. I hope you know how much I love you."

Before he can reply, I turn and walk into the closet to grab some clothes. As I do, more tears run down my face. I pray to God I can get them all out now, so when I'm at Glory's I don't show my emotions. Motherfucker, this is going to suck big time.

* * *

When we approach Glory's house, I see all kinds of vehicles in the driveway and around the house. As Noodles pulls alongside Panther's truck, I see Zoey leaning against Panther with Avalanche sitting right next to her. Oh shit, this is really bad. My bestie and enforcer usually doesn't show any emotions, and now she looks like she's about to break.

I get out and move directly to the truck my bestie is in. Avalanche steps out, grabbing me close while whispering to me.

"Tink, she's not doing good. I think she's thinking about how Hannah was when she found her, and now there's another kid out there in a similar situation. And she's worried like hell about you. Be gentle with her."

At first my temper starts to get hot until it hits me how much he truly cares for his brother and best friend's ol' lady. Damn, I wish I could find this raw diamond a woman. I give him a squeeze.

"Avalanche, she's lucky to have you as a friend and brother. Thank you for being there for her."

I hear the door open behind me and when I turn, Yoggie and Glory are looking out, confused. Before I can take even a step toward her, Olivia squeezes between the two of them rubbing her eyes. Then she looks up at the adults.

"Is this a party? Why so late? I'm tired."

Yoggie leans down, picking her up, saying something to his woman, then walks back into the house with Olivia. Pulling her sweater closer to herself, Glory must see something on all of our faces as she leans back against the front door. Feeling a hand wrap around mine, I know it's Zoey. Together we walk toward the house with all of our sisters falling in behind us. Well, until someone else grabs my other hand. When I look that way, I see Hannah facing forward but I can tell she's been crying.

Fuck, this is going to bring up all kinds of memories for my daughter and there's nothing I can do about it.

"Tink, what the hell is going on? It's what, holy fuck, it's three fifteen in the morning. Did someone die, oh my God, is it Momma Diane or Pops?"

I can't get a word out. My mouth is as dry as cotton, and I don't have a clue what to start with. Looking at Zoey, I can tell she's going through the same thing as me. I feel all my sisters closing in behind us. Glory is watching all of us closely and something goes across her face.

"Oh my God, is it Lilly and Gino? Did you find something out? Are they dead?"

That last sentence comes out barely as a whisper but is filled with such pain. Why does God do this to good people, while sick bastards live life with not a care in the world?

"No, Glory, that's not why we are here, but we do have some news."

As I'm talking, Yoggie comes back out, catching Glory as she almost falls right into him. Then he puts his arms around her shoulders, pulling her in. When he kisses the top of her head, I can hear just about every one of us sigh. When he looks our way, his eyes meet mine.

"Tink, can one or two of the prospects go sit in with Olivia? I'm getting the feeling that maybe we should take this to either the garage or pole barn. I'd appreciate it if Olivia isn't left alone. She's worried like crazy in there, so whoever goes in, she's been crying."

Before I can say a word both Peanut and Kiwi step forward.

"We got this, Prez. Yoggie, we'll keep her company. Do you want her to stay in bed, or can we maybe watch some television until she calms down? Also, how about some warm milk, might help?"

Hearing Peanut speak up, I can't believe how far she's come in the last year. I remember her when she first came to us, she barely looked at anyone let alone talked.

"Yoggie, yeah, probably the pole barn. It's bigger, if that's okay. Glory, just a few more minutes then we'll share with you what we found out tonight. And just so you know, I made sure those motherfucking bastards suffered until they took their last breaths."

Hearing Zoey's voice filled with emotion, I'm struggling not to start bawling, but Hannah squeezes my hand so tight my mind goes blank. I look at her and she is watching me like a hawk. I hold on to her hand, and we all start to walk to the pole barn. The whole way there I'm struggling to find the words that will undoubtedly break my VP's heart.

TWENTY-TWO
'YOGGIE'
SEBASTIAN

I can feel the mood between the Devil's Handmaidens sisters, not to mention the looks going between Noodles, Panther, and Avalanche. My gut is telling me my Bae's world is going to be torn apart. I catch Noodles's eyes and he shakes his head slowly. Can't stop to question him as I'm holding Nora up as we walk to the pole barn.

Once in, everyone walks over to what I've started to make into a man cave slash movie area. I have all kinds of seating due to the kitchen area I just finished and added a table and six chairs. So as everyone finds a seat, I walk to the refrigerator and pull out waters and put them on the table before repeating it again.

The way Tink is panicking and glancing at Shadow, who is actually looking like she might cry, scares the shit out of me. If that woman is emotional, might as well shoot me now. I've never seen her show a lick of emotions. Once everyone is sitting and looking around, Tink stands as do Noodles and Shadow. Panther and

Avalanche are standing against the wall close to Shadow. Oh, this is beyond bad, it's going to be earth-shattering. It dawns on me the entire club is here. Well, we might be missing one or two of the sisters, but damn near the entire club.

Surprisingly Shadow takes the lead, though Tink is right beside her. Noodles is now behind both of them, a hand on each of their shoulders. The men know already.

"Glory, as you know we had to work over some of those assholes at our trucking company. During that some shit came out and, unfortunately, it involves you. Now, as you can see, just about the whole club is here to support you in whatever you need. So not gonna keep you in agony. One of the men broke down totally and when I questioned him about Lilly, he did tell us she was at a compound but he didn't know which one. He did say they move her every couple of months from what they'd heard. Remember these are worker bees who are expendable. After working him harder, he told us that even if we found her, she wouldn't leave, no matter what. When I asked him why, he explained that no way Lilly would leave because she'd have to leave her child behind, and she would never do it."

Shaking my head, I know I didn't hear Shadow correctly. Glory is completely still, staring at Shadow with no expression on her face. One second she's almost comatose, then the next she's up and running toward Shadow. When her first punch hits Shadow, her nose bursts blood. Through the next few minutes Glory wails on Shadow, and not once does she try to protect herself.

I've never seen a woman just stand and take a beatdown like she is. What surprises me is that not one of the other women try to stop Glory but stand close, watching every swing, punch, and occasional kick.

When Glory starts to slow down, Shadow raises her arm to wipe her face but still not a word at all. I can already see her eyes turning black from the broken nose. Her lip is cracked and also bleeding. Then I hear Glory gasp as she takes in the damage she caused. Her bloodied hands cover her face. I walk over to her, pulling her back to my front. She instantly goes limp in my arms. That's when Tink comes over to us both. She grabs Glory's hands, hanging on to them.

"Sister, look at me. Now, Nora. I know what you are going through. No, you know I do. Don't get pissed off or draw into yourself. As hard as that was to hear, you know more than you did earlier. No, I'm not making light of this, just trying to put it into perspective. We can't do anything to change what's happened to Lilly up to this point. All that's left for us to do is find her, bring her and the little one back here, and help them both try to heal. You can do that and every one of us will help too. It's up to you but this I promise you; this club will not stop until the Thunder Cloud Knuckle Brotherhood is put to ground."

I can hear the emotion in Tink's voice and I feel the way Nora's body jerks with her words. When she pulls away from my body, I let her go because I know she wants to get to Tink. Watching them fall into each other, holding on tightly as they sob together, it takes but a second or two before Shadow and the rest of the women surround them. I look to see all the men looking anywhere but at the bunch of women holding on to each other.

Time passes and when I see that the women are not going to separate, I walk over to where Noodles, Panther, and Avalanche are now all leaning against the wall. When I get closer, Noodles pulls me into his side, slapping my back.

"Sorry, brother, for the intrusion but when Shadow beat the information out of them, she couldn't hold back. Then she called Tink and the rest you know. Watch out for your ol' lady 'cause this shit will hit her when she least expects it. These women are strong but it's that soft center we need to protect."

I nod before hitting the wall myself. Running my hands through my hair, I hear Panther and Avalanche whispering before the big man walks out. Panther leans out to see me next to Noodles.

"Avalanche is going to wake up the rest of our crew so they can start searching the area for any kind of unusual people around. Also, we have a pretty good nerd who can make a computer sing. He'll get to work on any of the brotherhood names we know of and try to find where they are right now. When it gets to be morning, I'll reach out to Ollie to see if he has any ideas of what can be done. He has connections, so between him and Tank maybe we can get an arial view to see if there's any movement in the rural areas. That's where this group tends to populate because they can then get away with the shit they are pulling. I'm also reaching out to a couple of my contacts in the FBI and CIA to see if they have any teams working on the Thunder Cloud Knuckle Brotherhood, and if so, what they've found out so far. Keep the faith, Yoggie, she's one of ours just like you are, and we protect our family."

Coming from Panther, a man I've admired since we first met, it hits me, the sincerity I hear in his voice. I've watched him and I've wished for some of his patience and humility. He is what he is and nothing more or less. Lives humbly and never have I heard him complain or bitch about shit. I believe it comes from his heritage but also because that's the man he wants to be. Trying to keep my emotions at bay, somehow, he knows and walks over to me, pulling me in tightly, giving me what I needed from a friend.

When he lets me go, he looks me in the eye but doesn't say a single word. I feel something move in me and suddenly my vision seems clearer and the weight in my chest seems to be lighter. I just return the stare, not sure what the fuck is going on. I've heard talk that both Panther and Avalanche are empaths, but this is the very first time I'm experiencing it. When I'm feeling calmer, he squeezes my shoulders then lets me go and moves back over next to Noodles.

I look over to the group of women. They are sitting at the table, have pulled the stools from the small island, and are in deep conversation. Nora seems to be holding her own, but time will tell. Honestly, Tink and Shadow look worse than my Bae. Hannah is glued to Nora's side, while I see Raven already pounding her laptop keys. Heartbreaker is making coffee while Wildcat talks to her, sipping on a cup of coffee, I'm assuming.

This night that started as a nightmare is shifting, so maybe something good will come of it. In the morning I'm gonna talk to Tank and Enforcer, get some outside insight. With all of us working together we'll find a way to rescue Lilly and her child. I also know, even though she's not said too much, Nora is worried about Gino. I'm not jealous in the least, if she wasn't I'd be worried, for Christ's sake. He was her husband and father to her children.

Figuring on giving the women their time, I walk outside, taking in some deep gulps of nighttime air, crisp and cold enough to chase away my tiredness. Walking toward the house, I figure to check in on Olivia. When I open the door, I quickly walk in and close it. On the sectional is a mound of blankets and all three are fast asleep. Peanut is lying down with Olivia at her side. Kiwi is at the other side with Olivia's legs over her lap. I can give this to Nora so she doesn't worry.

Turning, I start to go back out but first set the alarm. Then when I'm out, I lock the door. Can't be too careful right now. With my head clearer, I go back into the pole barn to see what's going to be the next step to ridding the world of this brotherhood. Time to get fucking serious and take care of business. I'm getting into my military mindset, which can be dangerous if it mixes with the biker in me.

TWENTY-THREE
'LILLY'

Not sure what's going on, but something is definitely up. When the old bitch came in to make sure I was in bed, well, where the hell else would I be? Come on, every night I'm cuffed to the bed frame, so really. If not for Angel I would've left and run away a very long time ago. My baby girl is the only thing keeping me here.

I remember that horrible night when I first got here.

Talk about being scared to death. Daddy told me we had to disappear and Uncle Oscar told him this was a safe place. Little did we know then how bad my dad's brother was. When we arrived, it seemed okay in my little girl mind. They took Daddy's car to 'hide it' and took us in and fed us. It was strange how none of the women talked or even looked us in the eyes. The men were way different. They had no problem staring at me like I was a piece of candy. Daddy even told the ugly man to quit staring. That got Daddy a fat lip because that man punched him right in the face and said next time he wouldn't be so nice.

Even as a small child I knew we were in big trouble. First Uncle Oscar took Mommy then told us to come here. Now they were being mean to us and even hit Daddy. When I started to cry the ugly man came to me, picking me up. That's when Daddy stood up and tried to grab me, but that's when it happened. I'll never forget it. The back door opened and there was Uncle Oscar. When Daddy saw him, at first I saw relief but then something really scary crossed over my Daddy's face. When he looked back at me, he mouthed, "I'm so sorry pumpkin."

When Uncle Oscar reached Daddy, he hugged him and for a quick second I thought it was okay. Until Daddy jerked and I saw the knife that was stuck in his belly. When Uncle Oscar jerked it up, Daddy's eyes rolled then he slumped forward. I started to scream but ugly man put his hand on my mouth, telling me to, "Shut the fuck up." Then he leaned down and licked my face.

Uncle Oscar pulled the knife outta my daddy, wiping it on his jeans. He stomped our way saying something to the man, who just laughed. When my uncle grabbed me, the man said a bad word. Then I was put behind him while I watched him pull a gun and shoot the man in his head. I closed my eyes and started humming like Mommy always told me to. There was a lot of people screaming then it went quiet when my uncle started talking in a weird way. Then he picked me up and walked away to a room that he said is where I would sleep. Then he said that he'd sleep with me. I looked at him and said, "I'm a big girl and can sleep by myself." He grabbed me and threw me on the bed. He started telling me how he tricked his stupid brother into thinking this place and the people were safe. Uncle Oscar said this was the most unsafe place to be if we had not been with him. Then the bad thing happened. I never talked to him again unless he asked me a question.

When I was, I don't know—eleven—I thought I was dying when I peed blood. The mean lady said I was a woman now and had to act like one. She dressed me up and put stuff on my cheeks and lips. That night while we ate dinner, Uncle Oscar told me that now we could finally complete our union. I had no idea what he meant but when, don't know, four months or so later I was really sick. Uncle Oscar got really happy and one of the nice older girls told me I was with child. Again, had no idea what that meant until my belly kept getting bigger, and I couldn't keep anything down in my belly. When I woke up in the middle of the night and my bed was wet and in so much pain, I thought I was dying, the old mean lady came in and between her and the other woman I had my little girl. She was perfect in every way. I wanted to name her Nora after my mommy, but wouldn't dare because all Uncle Oscar talked about when he did bad things was how if he couldn't have his Nora then I was a good second because I came from her.

Just those memories in my head cause me to feel sick to my stomach. Now Oscar is here less than ever and I'm so happy about that, even though I'm still in prison and don't get to have my daughter with me all the time. Besides that, I've come to accept my life ended when I was pulled from my parents because a very sick man was obsessed with my mom.

There are times when I allow my mind to wander and I wonder what my life would be like if my family was able to just be and go through life like a normal family. Why was my dad normal and my uncle was a sick asshole? The only good thing is that in this compound no one will come near me or touch me because I belong to Oscar. Over the years some have tried but didn't breathe for long once the maniac found out. And his punishments were brutal. From poisoning to asphyxiation, drowning, and torture. Now no one will even attempt to take a chance on me, so I live my life for my daughter. If I didn't have her, I would probably end my life because what I'm doing isn't even remotely close to enjoying my time on this earth.

In my early teens, when the pain was way too much for me to even understand, I started cutting and hurting myself. That is until Oscar caught me one time and slit my upper arm up so badly, I needed stitches. I stopped that night because he scared the shit out of me. And he threatened me that if I killed myself, Angel would take my place. That scared me and woke me up at the same time. I would never put Angel in danger and all she has to protect her is me. As long as I play along, she sleeps in the adjoining room. When I was having my tantrums, Oscar moved her down the hall in a dorm setting with other young girls. We both hated it and she would cry in my arms when they returned her to me every morning.

Sometimes late at night I wonder what my mom is up to and it eats at me why she never looked for me. For all I know she's dead too. Oscar never really talks about her unless he's drunk or high. Then he rants and raves about how my dad stole her from him. Whatever happened between the three of them, I should not have to suffer my whole life. I can never forgive him for all he's done, and if I ever get the chance, I'll kill him with my own bare hands.

Feeling the urge to urinate, I hold back. My chains don't reach the bathroom so there's a potty chair next to the bed. I try very hard not to use that but I have over the years, especially that time I was extremely sick with the stomach flu. That was horrible as I couldn't stop going potty, and I had to scream for someone to empty it because I had severe diarrhea. Talk about embarrassing but more I was so angry. Not sure why the need to keep me chained at night, we are in the middle of who the hell knows because I sure don't. And every few months they move me and Angel to a new location, so I don't even bother with the effort to try and make friends. It's useless because I won't be staying.

Knowing if I don't pee before I fall asleep it will bother me all night, I get up and take care of business. When done I put the plastic cutting board on top so it keeps any odors inside, hopefully. Yeah, I live like this and have all my life. But for Angel, I'll do it until I can get us away from here.

My last thought before I slip into a dreamless slumber is if my mom ever thinks of me, and if so, does she remember when we were happy, just the three of us? I hope if she recalls those times, it brings her happy vibes because it's those memories that keep me going day in and day out. That and my daughter.

TWENTY-FOUR
'TANK'

JAY

Soaking in our whirlpool every morning helps my arthritic body to move better. If I'm not in this one, I'm just in the tub with Epsom salts. Diane looked it up and you can't put the salts in a whirlpool, something about acidic levels. So if I need the extra jolt of Epsom salts I go in the guest bathroom and soak. Thank God we have four full baths and two half ones. Especially with Hannah still coming and going, and Ironside's parents are here while their house is being built. His sister and brother-in-law just finished their home and moved in.

My body is so relaxed, my head is back on the pillow Diane bought for me so I don't cramp my neck. I'm in between being asleep and awake and for once my mind is clear. I mean, as clear as it can be. So when a hard knock comes at the door, I immediately reach to the ledge for my gun. Before I even get a word out, I see Enforcer with a smirk and Yoggie, who's looking anywhere but at me, walking in. Goddamn, I can't even soak in peace anymore, for Christ's sake.

"Now what, you motherfuckers? What's so fuckin' important that ya are pounding on my bathroom door and it's not even nine o'clock in the goddamn morning. When do I get some downtime, you bastards?"

Yoggie looks guilty as hell while Enforcer goes right to the sink and hops up on the counter, getting comfortable. Yoggie goes up to the wall and leans against it, crossing his ankles and trying to look relaxed. Watching him, I can tell he's anything but relaxed. So seeing that, he's the one I go to first.

"Yoggie, break it down for me, brother. What's got both of your asses up here when you both have women in your bed now. I mean, if my choices are talkin' to you two bastards or being able to wake up to my ol' lady, I'll definitely pick option two. So talk."

"Well, Prez, ya know there was trouble last night. Well, Shadow and her girls got those assholes they caught to talk and, yeah, they confirmed that Lilly is alive, living in one of the compounds. Then they dropped a bomb, saying there is no way she will ever leave because she won't leave her kid at the mercy of those assholes."

My body jerks with what Yoggie just said. I can't sit in this spa any longer, I'm feeling sick all of the sudden. Grabbing the bar on the wall that helps me get up, I manage to do it without lookin' like an old fuck. When I go to grab my towel, Intruder has it spread out in front of me. Not sure what's up his ass today, but gettin' sick of his attitude. Until he looks at me with an expression I rarely see on his face. Insecurity and fear. Oh fuck, last time I saw it was when Vixen was in the hospital after they were attacked on the road.

Wrapping the large bath towel around me, I carefully get out of the tub, sliding my feet into the slippers right off to the side. Bathroom, though huge, is feelin' a bit tight, so I walk into the bedroom, go to the walk-in, and grab my robe. Once I have it on, I turn and look at the two brothers in my bedroom.

"Let's take this downstairs, brothers. I'll see if Diane can put some coffee on for us. Then I need the whole story because right now I wanna put to ground every motherfucker who touched that poor child. This is hitting way too close to Maggie's situation. Come on, no time to waste."

Goddamn, it's after breakfast and coffee that Diane insisted she make for the three of us. Then we sit in my home office, tryin' make sense of something that never will. Why the hell are the Thunder Cloud Knuckle Brotherhood keeping Glory's kid alive all these years? Something is sittin' way left with me. Diane has come in and out of the office with refills of coffee. On one of her return visits, she stops and listens to us talk. I see it on her face right before I ask her what's bothering her.

"Jay, from what I'm hearing maybe the uncle is way more involved and has more pull on that brotherhood than anyone ever knew. Someone should check to make sure the man in jail is actually Glory's uncle and this racist group doesn't have someone in his place. Once you know that, then get together with Maggie's club and try and figure out how to get that child and her baby out of there faster than I can say your favorite word, Jay. Now, husband of mine, get it 'fucking' done."

With that she turns and walks out as I watch her with my mouth open 'cause it dropped down. In all the thirty plus years we've been together and she's been my ol' lady, I could probably count on both hands how many times before today she used that word. And most of those times she had whispered that to me while we were in bed. My ol' lady, unlike all the females in my daughter's club, was raised during a different time. Not saying she don't swear with words like damn, shit, and bastard.

When I look at my two brothers they are also shocked. Enforcer's eyes are huge because he's been with us forever, and when he lived with Diane and me, she was strict when it came to language, being polite, and swearing. Many times when Enforcer, or back then he went by Travis, was young, Diane busted his chops for cussing.

"All right, close your goddamn mouths. I'm gonna do something I've not done in years. Promised myself I would never contact him ever again. Enforcer, ya know who I'm talkin' about, right? If anyone can help, I'm praying it's him. Let me make this call, get the brothers together. Then call Maggie, tell her the Intruders will be at the ranch around, fuck, I guess noon. Hopefully by then we can figure something out. Put Freak on this, tell him to find something, a camera with Lilly's face on it. Or complaints from innocents on racist bastards in their area or, I don't know, tell him to use his imagination. We need to have an idea where their compound is. Now, get outta here."

Once they're gone, I hit the walk-in closet and go to the huge safe on my side in the back. Opening it, I reach in and pull out a worn-out leather journal then go back in our bedroom, sitting on one of the chairs in the 'lounge area,' as Diane calls it. Fuck, she's the only one lounging here, always with a book in her hand. Shaking my head, I get back to the business at hand. Opening the book, I feel my soul tremble. Everything in this book is from a time I'd like to forget because I wasn't a good man. I did whatever was necessary.

Finding his name, I grab my cell off the side table, and punch in his number, then take a deep breath and hit call. Part of me hopes it goes to voicemail while the other part just wants to get this over with. Winner is voicemail.

"Hey, ya got Donovan Finnegan from Finnegan's Quest Sentries, better known as FQS. Leave a message with your name, number, and reason for calling. I'll get back to ya as quick as I can. Later."

FUCK!

"Donovan, it's Tank. Long time no talk, brother. First, congratulations on Finnegan's Quest Sentries. Glad to hear it's up and running for ya, brother. Reason I'm reaching out is I need to call in that marker or favor, whatever ya want to call it, 'cause I got a situation and only someone with your resources in all levels of our government might be able to help us. When ya get a minute call me back, and not being a bastard by being pushy but this is a volatile situation involving innocents. Thanks, Donovan."

With that I disconnect and just sit here as my mind goes back to when our club was workin' with Nova on that huge drug bust. Good for him, he deserves any kind of happiness since that incident went down. He's a good man just trying to live his life.

Feeling her before I even lift my head up, Diane is leaning against the doorframe watching me watch her. Then she starts to come my way. She puts her hands on my shoulders then pulls me into her body so my head rests on her belly. Damn, wish I could stay like this the entire day, but ain't gonna happen. So I give it to her.

"Gotta set up a meeting with Maggie for around noon. Then going into the clubhouse, want to touch base, see how shit is going. Babe, feel so outta touch lately. Must be getting old, Diane. Shit, I ain't even close to Medicare, for fuck's sake. I'm just approaching my late fifties, for Christ's sake, and I'm losin' it. Maybe I need to take those pills they're always advertising on the television at night. You know, if you're losin' shit and can't remember dick take one of these pills daily and they'll help. It's that or start taking those gummies everyone is talking about. Dr. Cora at the ranch told me they might help my arthritis. Think on it, woman, then give me your thoughts."

"Jay, you aren't losing it, husband, especially if last night was any example. What you're experiencing is the same stuff that both Maggie and Zoey are going through. None of you have had a break or time to relax and just be. It's drama after drama and one worse than the last. I'll talk to Dr. Cora about those gummies, and if she thinks they'll work then definitely a yeah from me. Now you need to go see Dr. Cora and get a physical because, Jay, I know you're not feeling good. Don't lie. So do we have a deal?"

How does she do that, always gets the upper hand? Probably because she's so much smarter than me. And my ol' lady is right, I'm not feelin' my best. So as usual she knows what I need before I do.

"You drive a hard bargain, but it's a deal. Let's confirm it with a kiss then gotta get ready and go, woman."

Reaching for her, I pull her down, and devour her lips like I've not had them in months, though it was only last night. When I hear that sound she makes that I love, I release her and stand.

"Now that should keep me on your mind, woman. Now get, gotta go. Hey, Diane…. Love ya, baby."

Her face goes instantly soft and she nods.

"Right back at you, Jay. Be safe, don't get dead on me. We have a date with our bed tonight. Now that should keep me on your mind, husband of mine."

With that she turns and sashays her way outta our

bedroom. Goddamn, I'm one lucky son of a bitch for sure. That draws a smile on my face as I get ready to take on the day. Damn, I hope it goes by smoothly and I'll be right back here tonight with my ol' lady in my arms.

TWENTY-FIVE
'YOGGIE'
SEBASTIAN

Ending the call from Tank, I look at my watch. Damn, gotta get my ass moving if I'm going to make it to the clubhouse. After the interruption of our evening, I was surprised at how well Nora handled the information Shadow and the club came to break to her. Everyone stuck around 'til they were positive she was okay. Olivia was fast asleep, so when Nora went into the bathroom, I gave her time. I heard the shower go on and was kind of surprised but figured she needed that feeling of clean. It wasn't until I heard the soft sobbing that I didn't even give it a thought when I opened the door, pulling my clothes off as I did. Walking into the shower, Nora was huddled on the shower floor. Kneeling in front of her, I gently pulled her into me. When her body started shaking, I could feel the anguish pouring out of her. Fuck, if I could, I'd tear Oscar's body apart with my own hands. Why? What the fuck went wrong with his brain that he thought it was okay to make his own brother choose between his wife and daughter? And then for Oscar to kidnap and keep his niece imprisoned while he physically and mentally abused her. *Unfortunately*, I thought to myself, *I couldn't change the past but I'll damn well do my best to keep her safe going forward. Well, right after we tear Oscar apart limb by limb.*

Not sure how long we stayed like that but my knees were burning so I gently lifted her up in my arms and shifted so my ass was not on the floor, and I was leaning against the shower wall. After a bit I felt her body start to relax so I continued rubbing up and down her back while putting small kisses on her forehead and head. When her hands started roaming my chest my body reacted immediately, so I was sure she could feel my hard cock against her ass, though not where I was going when I came in here. Was worried about her and just wanted to comfort her, that was it.

When she licked my neck, I was gone. *This woman owns me body and soul and now that we are able to truly be together it almost feels like we are new again*, I think to myself. God, I was becoming a pussy lately and if any of my brothers knew I was getting soft, they'd beat me silly. So into my head when her warm breath breezed against the head of my cock I almost lost myself and shot a load. *Damn it, I can never understand this thing between us. It's electric*, and that's the last thought I had because Nora was working me, and I was just feeling everything on the downslide and on the grip upward. Before I knew it that familiar feeling was happening all over me, while my balls pulled up tight to my body.

Before I could even warn her, my body let loose and I lost every thought as I just slid down the shower wall, my body drained.

"Sebastian, just so you know, I appreciate you. Thank you for always being here for me. My heart is shattered but we now know she's alive so that gives me a little hope. I'll search for her and the baby until I have no breath left in me. Tink did it with Hannah and look how that turned out. I've got to have faith. Now I'm hungry, so let's get off this uncomfortable as shit shower floor, rinse off, and go raid the kitchen."

Knowing she was trying to bypass how deeply she was upset, I pulled her on my lap while stretching my legs out. She sighed, probably thinking I was gonna try and make her feel better, but nope not where I was going.

"Nora, Bae, never doubt my feelings or how deeply they run. We will get through this and bring Lilly home, no matter how long it takes. Now, like you, I'm starving so move for a second and let me get up first."

I shifted and used the wall to help me push up with my bent legs. Once standing, I reached down and pulled Nora into me. We slowly washed off then got out, both drying ourselves. Once we were in our pajamas, holding hands, we walked out to the kitchen and came to a dead stop. Sitting on a stool was Olivia, staring off at nothing. A suitcase was standing up next to the chair. Nora grabbed on to my hand but said not a word. I think she was in shock. So I asked.

"Olivia, hon, whatcha doing up and sitting here by

yourself? And more importantly, why is there a suitcase down there?"

"I was thinking, that's all. When do you guys want me to leave? Maybe Tink will let me go stay with Poodles, if she'll have me."

My head jerked back on my body just as I felt Nora take a step back, totally shocked. Before I could even move my Bae was almost running to where Olivia was slumped over the counter, head in her hands.

"Cariño, what are you talking about? Why do you think we are going to make you leave? I'm so confused. You know we won't ever hurt you, so please explain to me what you're thinking. Please, child, because you look like you're in pain and that makes me feel your pain."

Olivia looked at first Nora then at me. Her eyes were so sad that I walked to them both, embracing them tightly. I felt the little girl lean into Nora, who then leaned into me. Then I put my two cents in this situation.

"Little star, I've told you before, no matter what, you will never be alone as long as both Nora and I are breathing. So did someone say something to you to upset you? If so, tell me who and I promise I'll set them straight. So, beautiful, what's going on?"

I watched as her eyes again looked at Nora first then me and her face started to turn pink. Then she dropped her head again, then in a whispered voice broke our hearts.

"I heard that you found out your hija is alive, so guess you don't need a cariño too. That's why I asked when you want me to leave, so there is room for your daughter since I'm not that to you. Remember you told me I'm not a hija, so that's why I think you'll send me away."

My Bae had tears rolling down her face and couldn't seem to talk. She was looking at me with such pain in her eyes, I figured I could try to explain to this child she was wrong.

"Olivia, look at me, beautiful. I believe Nora already told you that this is your home for as long as you want it. No matter who else comes and goes, that will not affect you. We both realize that you've not had a normal life since your parents were killed. Honey, we might not be normal in some people's eyes, but one thing you will come to figure out is that what we say is what we mean and we mean what we say. So, honey, get this in your head. We want you here with us. Dr. Cora also told Nora that you already started your therapy sessions. It will help, just give it a chance sweetie. Finally, Poodles is still recovering and with the little one, her hands are full. Maybe you can go help her one or two days a week after school when your homework is done. So are we good, cariño? We care about you, don't forget that."

Olivia pulled back from Nora and went to stand on the stool, which had me moving closer to her in case she slipped. Instead, she leaned over to me and kind of leaped into me. I wrapped her up and she put her arms around my neck, hanging on tightly. From my side I felt a warm body pressing into me. Then to our utter surprise Olivia shocked the ever-lovin shit outta the both of us.

"Thanks, Yoggie. It finally feels like I have a real home. I was sad that I might have to leave with Nora's daughter coming here. Not sure I should say this, but I've learned never wait to say how you feel so here goes. I love you both so much. And thank you for saving me and bringing me to your home."

"Cariño, I'm sorry that you had bad feelings. Like Sebastian said, we want you here and I hope you stay until you are all grown up. Also, I want you to know that you can always come to us if you are having issues, no matter what they are. So we were going to get something to snack on, are you by chance hungry?"

I watched her look at Nora like she hung the moon. Then she slightly smiled and nodded. That was my clue to find something to feed my girls. And that hit me in the chest. I was truly hooked on Olivia, even though she'd only been with us for a little bit. I loved watching her personality starting to come to the surface. The poor child was being starved of emotion and even though the women tried, this child needed normalcy and that word did not exist with Juice and his asshole crew.

Shaking my head, I looked to see Nora getting ready to make eggs or omelets. Little Olivia was right next to her on a stool, trying to help her out. When Nora lifted her head and saw me staring at her, she gave me a huge as fuck smile and that was when I knew, no matter what, we'd be all right. As long as we stayed open and communicated, we'd be good. Thank God.

TWENTY-SIX
'GLORY'
NORA

Sitting in the building we built to hold meetings in when not at the clubhouse, I'm waiting for, I guess, everyone to arrive. Sitting with most of the Devil's Handmaidens sisters, my mind is all over the place. Everyone is on edge and nervous as hell. I jump when my phone vibrates, but grab it and pull it out of my pocket. Looking down, I see Taz's name so I engage it immediately.

"Taz, is everything okay?"

"Yeah, Glory, we're good. I'm at the store with both Teddy and Olivia in tow. Just wanted to see if you guys needed anything since we're here. Text me what it is, 'kay? Oh, Tink knows I'm not going to be there as I'm the pencil pusher, so to speak, and mainly stay in the office. You can fill me in when I drop off Olivia tonight. Keep your chin up, sister, this too will pass."

I hear her disconnect just as I see both Tank and Tink walking in, being followed by Enforcer, Shadow, and a combination of both clubs. Also see Shadow's dad, Sheriff George, and Phantom from Blue Sky Sanctuary. I stay where I'm at as everyone takes a seat and gets comfortable. I know this is going to be a long as fuck meeting so I get ready for it, as I try to find a position that won't kill my back and ass.

My God, how much longer are we going to go over this? Freak and Raven have found some activity about sixty miles from here at an old homestead. Also, there's been someone at the De Luca compound not that long ago, but like Avalanche mentioned, we don't know if there are underground tunnels running all around there or if they have hidden rooms that people could survive in until they felt safe enough to come out. What I do know is, I have to go to the bathroom before I wet my jeans.

Standing up just when Tink calls for a break, I make a move for the bathrooms before everyone else gets the same idea. Once done, I wash my hands then throw cold water on my face, hoping to wake up a bit. After I get back to my chair, I remember that I didn't send anything to Taz. Shit, she's probably done shopping. Well, I can try to see if she replies.

After thinking about it, I send her a short list, just some major staples we are out of. Immediately I see the three dots and then I get a thumbs-up. Great, she's going to save me so much time. Totally love my sister.

Dozing because Freak and Raven are talking while pounding on the keys of their computer, my eyes catch it when I see Tank jump up, phone to his ear, making his way to the exit with Enforcer right behind him. Something tells me to follow him so I do quietly. When I get out of the room, I see him down the hall so like I've got to use the bathroom, I take a seat, trying to hear his conversation, but I am just getting snippets until Tank lets out a bellow.

"Goddamn it, Donovan, what the fuck? Yeah, even bikers have enemies, dude. I wouldn't have called you if I didn't need the help. Yeah, I remember, I was there too, along with my club so don't give me any of your shit. You gonna help or not?"

Hearing the anger and frustration in Tank's voice, I stand and once again give him some privacy as I make my way back into the room. I take my seat and start to fade again when suddenly I hear what I think is Enforcer's voice yelling. I jump up, eyes wide open to see everyone looking his way as he's glancing at his phone. He hits something and puts it to his ear before he starts again screaming into the phone.

Tank walks over to him, which has Enforcer showing his president the phone. The absolute fear on the face of one of the baddest motherfuckers out there tells me something really horrible is either happening, already did, or is on its way. And when Tank searches until he finds me, I'm guessing it's more of my bullshit.

Feeling a presence, I look around to see all the younger Devil's Handmaidens coming by my side. I've watched most of these women mature and find out who they really are supposed to be. Seeing them here now for me is like coming full circle. With me being preoccupied,

I don't see what, but Enforcer walks to the wall, punching it until Avalanche literally walks up to him, picking him up, and taking him outside. Jesus Christ, what is going on? That's when Enforcer's next words send a fear like no other because when he yells it aloud, he's looking directly at me.

"Shit going down in town. Gerald at the gas station saw a bunch of unknown men walking into the grocery store, right before gunshots were heard. The store is now quiet except for the occasional person crying and then a gun going off. Sheriff George is on his way, but last I knew Que was doing errands with the kids and then making their way down to the grocery store to pick up some items. My question is, why no one had her back, for Christ's sake? We talked about protection and not to go anywhere by yourself. Why the fuck is Que on her own? Someone explain that to me."

I'm out of my chair before it all penetrates inside. Oh my God, Taz, Teddy, and Olivia are all together. Who was supposed to have her back and didn't? Then I hear who it was and I start to run. The brother who was supposed to take Taz's back was Malice.

* * *

My God, we've never driven into town like the devil's hounds of hell but this is an emergency. As we make it down Main Street, you can see folks trying to see what's going on but also are frightened. When we come to the end of Main Street and turn left onto Juniper Avenue, the grocery store is at the end of the street. The cop cars in front let me know that this is no mistake, but seeing Taz's big SUV Enforcer bought her has me gasping for air. Fuck, they are still in there, I'm almost positive.

Sheriff George comes our way once we've all parked. He looks worried but I've watched this man go through so much lately, and he barely gets upset or crazy. He's a cool cucumber.

"We've got ourselves a hostage situation. There are probably at least twenty folks in there, along with some of those motherfuckers in the Thunder Cloud Knuckle Brotherhood. They must be close and know our little town because word is they drove in like they do it every day. Walked in and nothing until first one shot then another before all hell broke loose. Now we're all here, so let's figure out how we are going to get those people out."

Staring at the front of the store, I can't imagine what's going on in there and all I can do is pray that my sister Taz, lil' Teddy, and Olivia are safe in there and are brought out shortly. Otherwise, I'll never be able to live with myself if something happens to any of them.

TWENTY-SEVEN
'TAZ'
RAQUEL/QUE

We are scrunched in a stockroom behind a bunch of pallets. When I heard the first gunshot, knew we had to find a place that would keep us safe until the cavalry arrived. Well, the Devil's Handmaidens sisters and Intruder brothers.

Being in the back, I don't have eyes on what's going on and am responsible for two young children, who are beyond scared to death and for different reasons. My son because he's never been good at highly emotional situations and poor little Olivia. When whoever started screaming her name, she froze and wouldn't move. Her face showed the fear in her body and heart. If not for my Teddy grabbing her hand and pulling with all his might, she might not have moved. We got in this room and found a place for the three of us to hide. I have no idea what's going on but I reach in my purse, pulling out my SIG Sauer P365 X 9mm. Then I reach in again, pulling out an extra clip, putting that in my jeans back pocket.

Both kids are watching me closely so I take a deep breath.

"Not going to lie to either of you. Those are bad people out there, so no matter what you hear, I want both of you to stay together and here behind the pallets. Please listen to me carefully. I'm sure Enforcer and everyone else are outside already, so it's a matter of time before they come busting in. I want you two to be safe. Now I want you to crunch up in that corner and I'm going to throw these tarps on top of you both. Breathe slowly and stay as still as possible. I'll be back as soon as I can. I love you both. Now I'm going to see what's going on."

I can see the fear in my little boy's eyes as I'm sure this is bringing back a lot of bad memories. Then there's little Olivia, because I'm guessing whoever that voice belongs to is one of the jagoffs who was down in Mesquite because she turned white when she heard it. I smile at both of them and point to the corner. They both go into the far corner and I grab two tarps and a few of the moving blankets, throwing those back there with them and on the floor before them, so it looks like they were tossed there when done with.

I pray to God he keeps them protected. Before I venture out, I reach at the stone hanging around my neck, holding it for a second to try and ground myself. Thank God I had my chakra cluster on. After taking a few breaths, I move quietly to the door that leads back into the grocery store. As soon as I push the door open, I see a few townspeople crunched down at the end of the aisles. The woman who works at the post office turns and sees me. She puts up both hands with seven fingers up, for a total of seven. Then she starts pointing and showing the number on her fingers. I give her a strained smile then move past her, guessing that the Thunder Cloud Knuckle Brotherhood is hanging out in the more open front of the store.

I grab my phone, texting on our emergency text. Give them the information the other woman shared then tell them where the kids are hiding. I put my phone back in my jeans pocket before I start to move toward the front of the grocery store. The closer I get the voices are clearer.

"Motherfucker, we can't get stuck here. I don't care what you think you know, it's not time for us to make our point. No, we've not been told this has been sanctioned by the elders. Why are you laughing? You, of all people, know the rules and regulations. Didn't you help write them back in the day? Come on, Oscar, quit fucking around and let's try to get out of here. If you ain't going, I sure the hell am. This shit ain't gonna get me killed."

Did he say Oscar? I thought that bastard was in jail. Fuck, did we not check to make sure it was him? I thought we did. Then I hear a voice straight from hell.

"Motherfucker, you either stay with us or I'll send you straight to hell. I'm in charge not you, little prick. What's it gonna be?"

I don't hear his answer but I clearly hear the shot that echoes through the store. Oh my God, did he just shoot someone? I slowly walk backward until I am able to hide at the end of the aisle. I hear that voice again screaming for Olivia to come out, or else when they find her it will be twice as bad. We're totally fucked because there are too many of them and just me. I don't have any idea what to do next when I feel my phone vibrating, so I take it out, seeing that it's Travis. Oh dear God, he must be losing his ever-lovin' mind. I don't need to know that Enforcer is out in front.

Again, I pull my phone out and text Travis. Looking at the text, I hope he can understand because the thought of him rushing the front and being killed would tear my heart out of my chest. I push send and then put it back in my pocket. Looking around, I spot one of Sheriff George's older deputies I've known for years. He gives me the hands down then points to his side, which after he lifts his jacket, I see his service revolver. Next to him is one of the ranchers from just out of town. He already has a gun in his hand. As I look around, I see just about everyone is armed. Sometimes I forget that in Montana it's unheard of if you don't carry a handgun, rifle, or both.

Deputy Carl motions for everyone to stay where they are. He's on his phone texting, so I glance back where I left the kids, wondering if that was a good idea. Before I can even head back that way, I hear screaming and yelling from the storage room. I start to head back there when two huge motherfuckers, each carrying one of the kids under their arms come out.

My son is barely moving while Olivia is screaming,

trying to scratch and bite. Well, until the asshole stops and cracks her across the face. She immediately stops and starts to cry softly. I thought I was out of their vision but then one raises his gun and points it at her.

"Move your ass over here, bitch, right now, or I'll shoot that little mute right in front of you instead of selling him to the highest bidder. Come on, get over here."

I slowly walk to them, trying to make eye contact with either of the kids. Olivia's eyes are shifting right then left while Teddy looks almost comatose. How in the hell am I going to get both of them out of here without being injured? Why the hell does this keep happening? Though this time these two innocents are right in the middle of it.

When we make it to the front, the two men talking in the corner turn and when one of them sees Olivia, his face lights up and he starts toward her. By this time the two jerks release the kids and they are both with me. Pushing Olivia behind me, I wait until the freak is standing in front of me, his eyes shooting flames at me.

"Move your ass, bitch. I ain't messin' with you. That piece of meat is mine and I'm here to get her back. Now move your ass. Come here, my little sweetie pie. Come to Daddy."

Hearing that, it hits me right in the head that this is the prick who abused her in Mesquite. I take a step forward so there's room between me and the kids. Then I fake trip and as I go down, my hand reaches out and I clamp on to one of his balls, twisting just how Shadow taught all of us. I've never heard a man scream like that before. Not sure how but even with his ball trapped in my hand, he forms a fist and punches me on the side of my head.

I fly about three feet before I land hard on my side. My head is ringing and through blurry eyes I see him grab on to Olivia's arm and start to drag her away while she's screaming bloody murder. Then I see Teddy and my eyes almost pop out of my head. Somehow, he got ahold of one of my guns and it's in his hands, though he's shaking badly. I try to get up but I think something is broke or strained. The jagbag who was jerking Olivia around then sees Teddy.

So instead of showing fear, he starts to laugh hysterically.

"Come on, ya dumbass. Like you could even shoot that gun, let alone hit me and not your little girlfriend. Teddy, right? Well, Teddy, did Olivia share with you what she did down in Mesquite before she came to Montana? By the look on your face, I'll take that as a no. So man-to-man I'll tell you, aghhhhhh."

Olivia somehow got her little fingernails into his hand and locked them in. When he swings his hand, he throws her across the front of the store. That's when Teddy walks up to Olivia's attacker and raises the gun above his head, aiming it at the jerk's body.

"I promised Olivia that I would always protect her. You are a bad man and we don't need you here."

Before I can say a single word, my son pulls the trigger and within seconds the area between his legs is red with his own blood. My God, Teddy shot him in his junk. At the same time a shot can be heard outside. Moving as quickly as I can, I grab Teddy first then move to the right and pick up Olivia. Then I move my ass toward the back of the store, screaming for everyone to get down. Right when I hit the end of the aisle the gunfire starts, so I dive down, lying on top of the kids. I'll do whatever possible to protect both of them.

It's over before it began. I can hear all the voices I never thought I'd hear again, but one stands out when he bellows my name.

"QUE? QUE, WHERE THE FUCK YOU AT? WOMAN, CALL OUT."

"Travis, we are back here. We need EMTs for Olivia and maybe Teddy, gotta take a look."

I hear boots hitting the concrete floor and within a minute I'm being lifted into the strong arms of Travis. Seeing him, I lose it for about twenty seconds, then I beg him to let me go.

"Que, I told you I'll never let you go but I get it, check them out see if they're hurt."

I bend down to see Teddy has Olivia in his arms, wiping her tears away. She's turned away from him and he's looking at me with huge eyes.

"Momma, what's wrong with her? She won't look at me and all she's doing is crying."

"Teddy, I think she's worried about what you heard from that man. Lots of stuff happened when she was held captive and she had no way to prevent a lot of it. Give her time, Son."

I watch as my young son leans into Olivia, wiping her tears off. He pulls her hand to him, placing it on his heart.

"Olivia, don't worry. I don't care what happened in that bad house. You know how I feel about you, and I can't believe you think I'd be mad at you for something that wasn't your fault. If we are going to be boyfriend and girlfriend, we need to trust each other. Like my mom and Travis do, or like Auntie Shadow and Uncle Panther. It's over, Olivia. Come on, let's get you checked out."

Slowly she lifts her head, looking at Teddy. Then she puts her hand in his and together they help each other up. An EMT comes toward us and Teddy politely asks that he look at his girl. My heart just about breaks because my son is growing up so quickly. And he's learning from the best of the best. Travis, Tank, Panther, and Avalanche. Can't ask for more than that.

TWENTY-EIGHT
'GLORY'
NORA

Watching people walk in and out of the grocery store, I'm just standing on the sidewalk looking at each face that goes by me. I can't believe this just happened. What the fuck is happening to our country and world? For shit's sake, thank God Taz and the kids are okay. I'm waiting for them to come out, don't want to add to the mass number of people rushing the store.

Just as I see Taz's rainbow hair coming out of the door, her hanging on to Olivia and Enforcer having Teddy in his arms, I start to walk toward them when I feel a poke in my side.

"Well, well, well, if it ain't my dear sister-in-law, Nora. Before you even think to pull some of your karate bullshit, I'll pull this trigger faster than you can even take a breath. Now turn the fuck around and start walking to the parking lot, now, bitch. Ain't gonna tell you again. I've got this place surrounded and all it'll take is a signal and everyone you care about will be mowed down by multiple assault rifles. Give me your hands first let me put some bracelets on, then get movin."

That voice, my God, it can't be. He's in jail, has been for years. Or was he? Did we ever do a face-to-face to make sure it was him actually in the prison? Fuck! My mind is shattering as it hits me this could actually be happening and not just a bad dream.

I'm pushed toward a plain, light-colored pickup truck. The back door is opened and I'm being herded to the inside when he pulls me up short. When his front presses into my back, I feel the hardness of his junk and I feel the vomit rise up my throat. Oh no, not again. Not even thinking, I whip my head forward then back and slam my skull right into his face. I hear a crunch and he moves away enough for me to turn around. Even in handcuffs I am able to keep my balance enough to kick him in his balls and watch him go down.

I start screaming like a crazy-ass woman as I continue to kick him anywhere I can. His face, crotch, chest, and I even jump on his stomach. All the while the noises coming from him sound like a rabid animal. Hearing my name being yelled out, I don't stop screaming until someone wraps their arms around my middle actually lifting me away from Oscar.

"Bae, I got ya. No, calm down, it's okay. Nora, listen to my voice, woman. I GOT YOU."

Hearing that crazy as fuck laugh draws me back to him and I try to kick him in the face. By this time Shadow, Freak, and Rebel are holding up Oscar, who's bleeding from multiple places. When he leers my way, I see one of his teeth is gone. Good, too bad I didn't kick the rest out of his mule mouth. He's a fucking asshole and this time I will sit in with Shadow until we get everything we need.

"Way to go, whore. You just signed Lilly and Angel's death certificates. It's about time anyway, because your daughter is as much a pain in the ass as you were, only worse. I'm sick of hearing her whining and excuses for everything. Better this way. I'll find another, maybe little Olivia, though I've already had a taste of that pure little one. Delicious."

One moment Sebastian is holding me up, the next he's pushing me into Avalanche. I've never seen a person move so fast. One minute he was right in front of me, the next he has Oscar in a chokehold with one arm, while the other hand has reached between Oscar's legs, and in a blink of an eye my brother-in-law is wailing like a bitch. Not sure what Sebastian did but it's mighty painful for sure.

"I never want to hear you say that little girl's name again. In fact, I don't want to even hear your voice unless you're asked a question, you demented motherfucker. Now you can nod and we can move this on, or I can give you to Shadow, Rebel, and Wrench to play with for a while. No, I can see it in your eyes, Oscar, but, man, you have no idea what true pain is until they get their hands on you. So, what's it gonna be? Personally, I don't give a flying fuck. I've got my woman and daughter to worry about."

Never have I heard a man say anything better than what Sebastian just did. I slowly, with the help of Avalanche, make my way closer to my ol' man. He turns for a quick second then gives his full attention to Oscar, who's smirking.

"Yeah, that's right, you limp dick asshole, keep leering. Enjoy it while you can. You have no idea what torture truly is, asshole. I've lived it for eighteen months in the Middle East. The things I can do would blow your mind. So, tell me where you have Lilly and the others or else, believe me, when I start you'll be begging me to stop or just end ya. That ain't me bragging that's me warning you. So, what's it gonna be, Oscar, 'cause you're at the end of the line asshole, just sayin'."

I see Sheriff George walking our way and for a split second I worry, until I realize who he truly is. And that he's also Shadow's father. When Oscar starts yelling and screaming about his rights our sheriff walks right up to him, slapping him a couple of times in the face, then pulling handcuffs off his belt, jerking Oscar's arm behind him, and cuffing him.

"Deputy Yoggie, please make sure the prisoner gets what he deserves. I mean, transported to the station. Now be careful because I hear the roads between here and the station are in really bad shape. I trust you to do what must be done, just like when you killed that brother from the Thunder Cloud Knuckle Brotherhood for harassing Glory over there. Thank God you have a badge, lets you handle the worst of the worst so our town can stay safe. I'm gonna get these assholes processed also. Seems like they are from that brotherhood, trying to make a diversion so someone can attempt to grab and hurt one of our own. Well, mister, look at me, you scum of the earth. I know what you did to that woman right there, so if you disappear and I don't ever have to see your face again, I'm good with it, and I'll sleep just fine. Thanks, Yoggie, for the help. I'll be up to my neck with paperwork on all of those still breathing from the store. And for such 'badasses' they can't stop running their mouths off about where they're hiding out, the women there, and this asshole here, so he's got nothing we need."

Shadow steps up and puts her arm on her dad's shoulders for a split second.

"Thanks, Dad, appreciate it. I might need to step in and give a hand to Yoggie, since we've not had any club business because of the brotherhood. First, let's find out where their camp is so we can see who needs what. But before I go, need to feel that flow of blood I love so much on my hands."

With that she goes right up to Oscar and right before my eyes she cuts off a part of his ear. Damn do ears bleed, because it was pouring out of him while he howled like a bitch. Then my sister Shadow grabs my hand and starts to pull me away. I turn to see Yoggie and Avalanche pushing Oscar toward an old truck that has Ironside behind the wheel. They literally throw Oscar in the bed of it and use bungee cords to secure him. Oh, that's not gonna be a good ride to wherever he is going.

"Not far, Glory, to our clubhouse and my wet room. He's going on ice until we can figure out and maybe find your daughter and granddaughter. Like Sheriff George said, those other jagoffs he was with are running their mouths off like you wouldn't believe. Come on, maybe we can get something to guide us because, for fuck's sake, there's too much area to go over with a drone or two. I know that Pops's friend and his crew are on their way right now from the airport to Timber-Ghost to lend a hand. And according to Pops, they have some 'interesting tools' they use to track criminals and find victims. Donovan, Pops's friend, said to put your brother-in-law on ice, literally, and they'd do the rest."

Before I can say a word, I see Olivia looking around from the ambulance. *Oh shit*, I think as I start to run toward her. She stands and when I'm just about to the ambulance she jumps right into my arms. Oh God, this little girl gave me the scare of my life today.

"Hija, my God, are you alright? I was so scared that something would happen to you, Teddy, or Taz. Is everyone okay?"

Looking down I see Olivia staring at me, her mouth wide open. Did they hurt her, for Christ's sake? I'm rubbing up and down her back and she lifts her little hands to grab my face. She's got tears running down her little cheeks too.

"Olivia, what's wrong, sweetie? Talk to me, you're scaring me."

From behind, Shadow comes closer and whispers something in my ear. My head jerks back, thank God my sister moved or I would have cracked skulls with her. The same shocked look is on Olivia's face but nothing, she's mute.

"Come on, sweetie, talk to me or does the cat got your tongue?"

That brings a tiny smile to her face as she leans in tight to me, wrapping those tiny arms around my neck.

You called me Hija. Why? 'Cause you said I was cariño, which means sweetie. Now you call me both. I'm confused."

"I'm sorry, Olivia, I was wrong. Yes, you are my sweetie, but more importantly you are my hija. Daughter, if you'll have me, well, me and Sebastian. We want you in our lives forever, so that's up to you. No, I don't expect you to decide now but put it on the back burner, something to think about."

"Will I get to call you Mommy and Yoggie Daddy?"

I hear the intake of breath behind me and smile to myself. Yeah, badass Shadow isn't fooling anyone, that's for sure. When she squeezes my shoulder, I glance back and see her smiling before she turns and walks away.

"Yeah, Olivia, if you want, but again that's your choice. Now let's get you checked out, make sure you are all right."

When she squirms to get down, I put her on down and instantly Teddy is at her side, grabbing her hand. She looks his way and smiles. My God, what happened in that store?

"My son saved your daughter, sister, that's what happened. We need to get them both checked out as they've been roughed over. Did I hear correctly, they caught your psycho brother-in-law? I hope to Christ maybe you can get some answers."

I grab Taz's hand, squeezing it tightly. I can feel the emotions rising up in me so it takes me a minute or two to say what I need to say.

"Sister, can't thank you enough for watching and guarding her today. I'll forever be in your debt and if you need anything, ever, you just ask, okay?"

"Glory, no need to thank me. Don't forget I had my heart in there too. All I can say is thanks to the powers that be everyone got out unharmed. Believe me, I'll be burning some sage tonight to get rid of the hatred that was thrown at us today. Now come on, these poor EMTs have been waiting for us to get our asses in gear. Kids, want to ride in an ambulance?"

All I hear are screams of yeah and it amazes me how resilient kids are.

TWENTY-NINE
'YOGGIE'
SEBASTIAN

I'm sitting in a lawn chair outside of an old log cabin in the back section of Tank and Momma Diane's property. Half of these people I don't even know, but because of how close I am to this shit because of Nora and her past with Oscar, Tank wanted me present, so here I am.

When the group of ex-military showed up in a darkened SUV, at first you would have thought it was a politician. Mayhem, the first man out, was huge and had a look about him that made me think of Shadow and Wrench. Then Donovan 'Nova' stepped out and I knew instantly he was Tank's friend. Power exuded off of him. He never looked around but I bet if you asked him, he could tell you how many of us there were and even what we looked like. He went directly to Tank, pulling him in, not for man pound on the back but for a true hug. Then he stepped back and punched my president's arm.

"Tank, 'bout time you reach out for some help. You

asshole, took ya long enough. Give me what you got while I have my team set up. I put a call out to one of mine at Ollie's to meet us here. She's one of the best at this kind of shit. Think she already worked with your girl, Shadow. So this is the connection you have to the Thunder Group Knuckle Brotherhood? Good, 'cause I've got a ton of shit to share with you too on that brotherhood. We've had a breakthrough with one of our own in their midst. Yeah, can you believe it, though I worry about that brother. Where can we talk?"

They walk over to the firepit that Tank had the prospect clean up and place chairs and a table there. The fire was actually burning low to keep the damp and cold down. I don't move, just keep an eye on everything. Feeling eyes on me, I look up to see some dude staring at me with those dead eyes. What the fuck is his problem? Then the huge guy calls out.

"Coma, get the lead out now. Grab those boxes, let's get this shit set up. COMA, now."

The dude abruptly turns and walks to the first SUV, grabbing a metal box that looks heavy. I was gonna offer but thought not my farm, not my jackasses. That thought brings a small smirk to my face. I grab my phone to check in with Nora and the kids. Seems like Teddy stepped up to the plate and went beyond to protect our Olivia. I owe that lil' man a lot.

"Yoggie, get your ass over here, brother."

When Tank bellows everyone listens, so I get up and walk over to where Tank, Donovan, and a few others are sitting. Tank motions me to sit at his left, which is generally for Enforcer. He's with Taz, Nora, and the kids at the hospital so they can all get checked out. Freak is walking up to us with his laptop, tablet, and a square box thing, along with his messenger bag. He plops down next to me and starts up his laptop. I'm watching, wondering if he thinks that he's going to get a signal. Then he opens the box and pulls out some kind of antenna. He messes with it for like two or three minutes, pounds on his laptop keys, then looks to Tank and nods.

"All right, first let's get the intros done. I called in a marker from one of the best, if not the very best, to help us with our problems. First, we need to locate Glory's daughter. Next, we need to have a plan in place so we can start the process of dismantling that racist piece of shit group of assholes. So, goddamn, this sounds like we're in school, for Christ's sake, but let's just go around and introduce ourselves."

I watch as everyone gives their name and specialty. Totally ex-military. When it is my turn, I do the exact same. Nothing more, nothing less. When introductions are done Nova starts asking Freak to put in coordinates. Every time Nova tells Freak to mark, my brother looks at either Tank or me but he does it. Finally, after the last one Nova asks Freak where the last coordinate is. Freak looks a little green around the gills.

"Well, uhmmm, it looks like it's well…"

"Goddamn motherfucker, Freak. Just give the man what he asked for, for Christ's sake. What's wrong with you today, brother?"

I watch our computer nerd look down at his

computer then at Tank, giving him big eyes. Jesus Christ, I lean over and check out his computer. When I see what it's showing, I immediately understand Freak's nervousness.

"Tank, looks to be the last four or five coordinates all are within an hour or so from town. Though the last one is your house, Tank."

Tank jumps up and as old as the motherfucker is, he can move. Well, that's what I thought until he grabs his chest as all the color leaves his face. Nova, Mayhem, and I make it to Tank right before he starts to fall to the ground. I start barking orders 'cause we don't have much time.

"Someone grab one of those SUVs, bring it as close to us as you can. Freak, put a call out to Momma Diane, Tink, Squirt, and Shadow. Let Enforcer know too. Everyone meet at the hospital."

Nova is watching me as I rip open my president's T-shirt and put my head to his chest. I can't hear a goddamn thing. I put two fingers on his neck and, yeah, at first thought I felt a faint pulse but then absolutely nothing. I start compressions while they bring the vehicle closer.

"Knock down the back seats, Tank's a big dude. Grab that moving blanket. All right, let's flip him to his side, all right, need as many bodies as possible. We need to get his ass up in that back end." In the end, all it took was Mayhem on one end and a few of Nova's team on the other. When I go to get in the back with Tank, Coma comes my way, pushing me toward the front.

"You drive, Yoggie, I got Tank. No, I got Tank, go."

Not sure of this brother, I have no choice since none of them live here in Montana. Freak jumps in the passenger seat and we take off. Thank God Malice is there to get them to the hospital.

"Coma, how's he doing? Can you take a pulse, dude?"

"Yoggie, he's as stable as he's gonna be. He's breathing on his own, but I flipped him to his side to keep his passages clear. Just get us there as fast as you can."

With Freak on the phone, now that we have a cell signal, I'm driving like a maniac. Can't let anything happen to Tank. Too many folks care about the old dude, one of them being my Bae. Not trying to think too much about all who care for Tank, I make it to the hospital in half the time. As I fly to the emergency room entrance, I see Enforcer, Panther, Avalanche, Tink, Squirt, Momma Diane, and Shadow all already waiting with brothers of the Intruders pouring in.

With everything else going on, the thought of losing Tank, one of the few men I respect, has my heart heavy. As we stop, the back is opened up and I watch in awe as Avalanche, Panther, and Enforcer pull Tank out, putting him on a gurney. Momma Diane is right at his side as they wheel him in. Freak jumps out to follow the crowd but turns and looks at me, fear in his eyes.

"Yoggie, good job, brother. If I ever need someone who keeps his cool in a real shitty situation, it's you, bro. Take a minute, come in when you can."

How the fuck that nerd knew I needed a minute don't know, but I thank him in my head. My own head is down on the steering wheel when my door opens and I feel a hand on my shoulder. Looking up, I see Panther with Avalanche behind him. Goddamn, these two are always together it seems.

"Come on, Yoggie, let's get you inside. Glory's inside with the kids, go on in, I'll take care of the truck. I gotcha, brother."

Avalanche saying that hits me in the gut. Fuck, what is wrong with me, for Christ's sake? I've fought in wars. Panther leans in.

"Sebastian, it's called emotions. A lot has been going on for both you and Glory. Take the help that's being offered. Come on, let's get you inside. Avalanche, go pick up those boxes of coffee, we're going to be a while. I gotcha, Yoggie."

While Panther and I walk into the hospital, Avalanche leaves to grab some coffee to-go boxes from Dunkin' Donuts. The entire time all I can think of doing is praying that everything works for my prez, my friend, and the only man who acted like a dad to me.

THIRTY
'GLORY'
NORA

I'm sitting in the waiting area with Olivia on my lap and Teddy next to me, him holding on to her hand. She's already bruised up from the grocery store incident, as is Teddy. Everyone is worried about Teddy, and Taz has already reached out to the therapist Momma Diane takes him to in Billings. It was agreed upon that tomorrow Teddy and Olivia would do a Zoom call with the therapist. Also the new one, Joan, at the Blue Sky Sanctuary is going to sit in with the kids too.

Now we are all waiting to see how Tank is doing. *My God, talk about bad fucking luck,* I think to myself. I don't believe like Taz does with her crystals or how Panther and Avalanche do with their Great Spirit. I do sometimes believe in people manifesting bad things to happen to others. And that's the feeling I'm gettin' lately. Our club has had a shit ton of unbelievable bad luck. I look around to see Momma Diane trying to comfort all three of her daughters: Tink, Squirt, and

Shadow, though only one, Tink, is her daughter and one, Squirt, is her granddaughter by blood. Shadow has been brought in and adopted by the family many years ago. Tink seems to be holding up as is Squirt, the one I'm worried about is Shadow. She is a total mess.

The outer door slides open and I see both Panther and Yoggie making their way in. My man looks totally out of it, so I carefully place Olivia in my seat next to Teddy. I look at Peanut across the room and she immediately comes to sit with the two lovebirds. Walking to Yoggie, I can see something's off with him. I glance at Panther, who gives me a shrug, but continues to be a support for my ol' man.

"Sebastian, come sit with us. Thanks, Panther, for bringing him in. They say that some news should be coming to us shortly, babe. From what I hear, you saved Tank's life."

"Yeah, he sure the fuck did."

I look to the left of Yoggie and see it's one of Tank's friend Nova's men, think they call him Coma. I just give him a smile then grab Sebastian's hand, and we now are sitting two seats away from Olivia. I move in close to my ol' man, who wraps me up good. I can feel him trembling so I wrap my arms around his waist.

Not sure how long we sit like this, but when the doors swing open from the back of the emergency room and three doctors come out looking for the family of Jay Rivers, just about the entire room stands up.

The doctors look around then back to Momma Diane.

"You want all these people to know your husband's status, ma'am?

Momma Diane shifts and turns around before she faces the doctor.

"This is my husband's family, so yes. Can you now tell me how my husband is doing?"

"Well, he's a very lucky man. Whoever made sure he was getting oxygen probably saved his life. Now, we had to do an angiogram to make sure there is no blockage. He has a little but we were able to do an angioplasty which opened it up and allowed blood to flow. He could use to lose a few pounds and eat a bit healthier, but I think this was a warning from his body. The man needs less stress in his life."

That comment has a bunch of us chuckling or cackling until the other two doctors stare at us.

"Bottom line is, Jay's gonna have to start taking some cardiac medications. Change up his diet and maybe try to get some exercise in the picture. What does he do?"

Leave it to Shadow to answer that question the only way she could. Smart-ass.

"He's the president of one of the most badass clubs in Montana. You're talking about Tank from the Intruders."

All three doctors look at each other, then at the group of people before really seeing all the kuttes everyone is wearing. The one talking to us smiles at Shadow for a brief second.

"Yeah, I've heard of Tank, just never had the pleasure to meet him. His club is responsible for our new cardiac care unit. I'll have to thank him when I check on him in a bit. For now, only immediate family to see him. Yeah, I get it, you're all his family but his wife and daughters, please? If everything pans out, he should be home in the next couple of days. Any questions?"

"You ride, Doc?"

I can't make out the female's voice but I hear snickering.

"Well, actually I do. Got a couple of Harleys and a BMW."

"Well, next time you're looking for something to do, give me a call, I'm always up for a ride."

Then I see her, it's Raven. When she walks up to the front, I see the doctor squint his eyes just a little bit before a huge grin hits his face. Can't say the same for Raven.

"Well, lookie here, it's little Brenna O'Brien. My ma told me she was talking to your ma and she mentioned you were in the girl club of bikers. How you doing, my little magnolia?"

The other two doctors shake their heads as they go through the swinging doors. Raven is beet red in the face and seems like she wants to run away.

"I can't wait to tell Dusty I saw you. I know he's wondered about you over the years. You two should give it a second go, Brenna, he's a good man, you know that. Can't believe everything you hear."

With that he turns and disappears behind those swinging doors. Raven, with her head down, moves quickly to the exit doors though Dotty and Dani are quick to follow. *Now there is a story for another time*, I think to myself. The jokester has some secrets of her own it appears.

Now that Tank is settled, I turn to look for Yoggie. He's by the door talking to Tank's friend, Donovan. They look to be involved in a deep conversation so I walk over to them. Donovan puts his hand out, introducing himself to me. Then nothing. Well shit, that ain't happening since it's my life they are fucking around in.

"So what had you two in such an intense conversation? Guys, I'm a VP of a motorcycle club, give me some credit. And this is my life that started this fucking mess, so spill."

Yoggie comes to me, pulling me into his side, then leans down and kisses the top of my head.

"Nova was explaining to me that they have about ten different coordinates that might be where Oscar and the brotherhood are hanging out. It may also be where he has stashed Lilly. So, they are going to check each one out and will get back to us if they find anything. And no, he doesn't want or need our help."

"Not sure I like that we have no option to tag along. This is actually my—no our—bullshit to deal with, even though Tank called you in for some assistance, Nova. What gives you the right to take over?"

"Glory, the U.S. government gives me that right. And since this involves that motherfucking racist group responsible for too many horrendous crimes, I have the authority to do just about anything. Now, like I was explaining to Yoggie, I'll keep ya in the loop. Glad to hear Tank is gonna pull through. He's a tough old bird, that's for sure. Tell him I'm around if he needs anything. Get some rest, Glory, been a trying day, that's for sure. Oh, on a separate note, you don't have to worry about Oscar any longer, that threat has been neutralized permanently."

With that he turns and walks away. Wait, did I hear him correctly? What did he say, they neutralized Oscar? What about Lilly? I run after him and call his name. He turns to face me.

"Nova, if you neutralized, as you call it, Oscar, what about my daughter Lilly and her daughter, my granddaughter?"

"Oh shit, sorry, Glory. We have three locations that we've been given so they are top priority. I'll let you know after we search each one. Don't get your hopes up just yet, let us do our jobs. Okay?"

I nod and he again turns and walks away. I watch for a minute or two, then walk back into the hospital to tell Yoggie what Nova just shared. Is it even possible that I might be able to hold my daughter Lilly soon? I can't even conceive that thought.

THIRTY-ONE
'GLORY'
NORA

It's been four days since Nova told me they had a lead on Lilly. Then radio silence. Tank is back home under the watchful eyes of Momma Diane. When Yoggie, Olivia, and I went to visit him, thought he'd jump out of his skin. Everyone was warned no sweets or snacks, no chew and no booze. I mean, what does that leave us to bring Tank? So Yoggie came up with the idea that he and Olivia worked on for a couple of hours last night. Watching Tank's face when he opened the handmade card from our family was priceless.

Olivia was so proud and had to show her 'Grandpa' all the different things she drew on the five-page get well card. There were his dogs and his bike. Him and Grammy. The entire family, which turned into a bunch of stick figures because there are way too many of us. Though her heart was in the right place. I acted like I didn't see Yoggie sneak in Tank's favorite, a bag of plain M&M's, in. That brought a huge smile to his face.

Now Olivia is at Taz's so she and Teddy can plan their wedding. Not going there today. Yoggie got pulled into an Intruder meeting to discuss what's gonna go on with Tank out for a couple of weeks. Yes, that was also Momma Diane's demand. She told her husband either he take the time off or just take off. He obviously picked the right choice.

I'm sitting in the family room, my Kindle to my right and the television on low, drinking a cup of coffee. I don't know what to do with myself. I've already cleaned the house, done laundry, and have dinner started. Been online looking in the shelters for a puppy or dog for Olivia. Ollie told me to stop by the Blue Sky Sanctuary if I want, as they just had two litters of puppies dropped on them. And literally he means they drop the boxes off and left. Total assholes.

Just as I take another swallow of coffee my phone rings, and I don't know the number. Usually, I let it go to voicemail but since Nova and his team are still out there looking, I grab the phone, engaging it.

"Hello."

"Hey, Glory, it's Nova. How ya doing?"

"Fine, Nova, any news yet?"

I hear him sigh, which tells me no good news for me. So, I wait to see why he's called.

"Not yet, Glory, we kinda got our hands full. Was calling to see if we could get some help from your club. The first location was filled with victims who were just left. We're thinking word got out about the grocery store attempt and the brotherhood pulled back from there. We need somewhere to place these women and children. Can you check with Tink and let me know, please. Tomorrow, we go to the second location. I hope to God we don't find this again. Glory, we found a shed that was filled with bodies. I mean, I've seen shit from all over the world, but in our own country? Shit, sorry, just tired, I guess. Again, just let me know, please."

Nova sounds beat to shit. If you're not used to the atrocities that occur in our world, especially here in the States, it can mentally and physically exhaust you. That's what he sounds like. War atrocities are much different than what is being done to women and children in our own country.

"Nova, don't hang up, man. Damn, are you direct and right to the point. Yeah, we can help out, bunkhouses aren't even close to being full. Let me check with my sisters, can you give an idea of how many and how bad they are?"

As he starts describing the conditions he found these folks in my heart starts to break. Here we go again, because when people are taken this low there are times we can't bring them back. That's the hardest thing the Devil's Handmaidens can't accept, but we're learning we can't fix everything, even though we try to. The thought also crosses my mind that I hope and pray Lilly isn't living like this.

* * *

It's another two days before I hear from Nova again. This time in person because his entire team is at the ranch dropping off thirty-five women and fourteen children from the first prison the brotherhood was running. It's all-hands-on-deck as we start our long intake process. To protect not only the survivors but ourselves, each person is carefully interviewed so we can obtain information. Then they are given a full physical exam and now we can add the emotional and mental exam, thanks to Ollie's therapist, Joan. Finally, we get everyone set up in the correct bunkhouse. With residents in them now, between Cynthia and the prospects, someone needs to be present in there at all times. We can also use Ollie's military folks who are waiting to get into Blue Sky Sanctuary. They are staying in the farthest one as guards.

It's taking twice as long because these folks have been in a form of isolation and they are scared, tired, and don't want to believe they are finally free. We have to be patient and give them time to acclimate to their new surroundings. Since we do this often, every time we bust a trafficking circuit, we're like a fine-oiled machine.

Yoggie, Olivia, and Teddy are helping with the food, watching some of the women and children crying when they are handed a sandwich or a piece of fruit. One little boy looked at Teddy like he was a superhero when he gave him a carton of chocolate milk.

"Bae, how you doing? My God, I had no idea all that your club does to help people through the next steps."

"Sebastian, this is just the beginning. Once a person

is settled and has started therapy, we talk to them about what they think they want to do. We pull in experts from across the country to help them learn to live on their own. Now, some don't want to and elect to stay here and make the ranch their home. Then they are trained on whatever job they want to do. How to receive a paycheck and live within their boundaries. Budgets and checkbooks. Personal hygiene, washing clothes, and going to a doctor or dentist. Things we all take for granted. When people are made victims, they lose all of these skills and have to relearn them to be part of society. Sorry, didn't mean to babble on and on. Oh, thanks for your help today. We are going to have some long weeks ahead of us, but I'm glad we're giving Nova some assistance. I mean, what would happen to these people if we didn't step up?"

"Bae, come here. I'm so very proud of what you women do. And everyone who comes through here will be a better person because of the Devil's Handmaidens' care. Now I was going to take Olivia and Teddy back home and get started on dinner. You need anything before I go? We might even go sneak in a visit to Tank. I hear he's being a beast, doesn't want to sit around wasting his life. Those are his words. Maybe seeing the kids will mellow him out for the rest of the night."

As we figure out our plans for the evening my mind drifts, wondering what Lilly is doing at that moment. These thoughts are driving me insane, though there's nothing I can do.

THIRTY-TWO
'YOGGIE'
SEBASTIAN

My body is screaming from using muscles I've not used in a while. The last week or so I've been taking care of business at our clubhouse, trying to make sure nothing slips by us with Tank down and out. I'm also very involved with keeping him in the loop and asking for help on shit like paperwork I don't know anything about.

All the brothers have been pretty cool. Well, with the exception of Malice. Something crawled up his ass and died. He's been a major dick to everyone for quite a while now. Nora's right, it's from when he went off on Tink and she whipped his ass. Why I'm blessed today to get his attitude, don't know, but I've had enough.

"Brother, what is your goddamn problem? Either be a man and step up to the plate so we can deal with it or get the fuck outta here."

He looks at me all snarky like. Whatever, I don't have time. Need to get to Taz and Enforcer's place before four thirty because the kids have a Zoom with their therapist, who wants all of the parents to be on this video call. When Olivia and Teddy asked me to come, I was shocked, though I think I hid it well. Told them definitely and I don't plan to break it. Didn't catch Malice's reply, so I ask him to repeat it. A mean grin appears on his face.

"What, sucking up to Tank ain't enough, now you gotta get in tight with Enforcer? For someone who just got a patch, your movin' up the ranks pretty goddamn fast. Don't leave much for the rest of us."

Since I don't have a clue what he's talking about, I just ask him.

"Malice, don't have a clue what your rantin' and ravin' about. I'm just trying to help out because our prez is out. That's it, I'm not asking for anything else. And for your information, 'brother,' I don't suck up to anyone and definitely don't kiss ass."

Before I can say another word my phone rings and when I look down, I see Nova's name above the number. I give Malice a wait finger and pick up the call.

"Hey, Nova, whatcha need, brother?"

"Yoggie, my God, brother, I don't believe my eyes. I need you to get here as quick as you can. Come alone, and don't say a thing right now. Anyone around you?"

"Yeah, I'm in the clubhouse, a bunch of brothers are here. Actually, was just talking to Malice, but it can wait. I gotta go to Tank's, need his help with some shit. Then the kids have therapy. Yeah, okay, I'll tell Tank when I see him. Talk to you later."

"Malice, gonna have to catch you later. If I don't leave and get Tank to go over this shit, I'll miss the kids' therapy. Just back off, brother, I'm not trying to step over anyone. Later."

I don't even give him a chance to reply but walk right to the bar area, grabbing the bunch of files I laid down. I walk outta the clubhouse to my truck, get into it, and throw the files on the passenger seat, reaching for my phone.

"Nova, I'm in my truck. Where am I going?"

"Yoggie, check your texts. I sent coordinates. I have no fucking clue where we are in the middle of fucking nowhere. It's about thirty-five minutes from the ranch. I'll be waiting."

What the hell is with all the secrecy shit? I want our lives to get back to the normal crazy 'cause this level of insanity is wearing me down. Nora and I are finally settled from the grocery store bullshit and Oscar. My Bae had to talk to the therapist a couple of sessions because the nightmares came back in full force after that son of Satan was disposed of like the bastard he was. I can't imagine all the damage Oscar has caused over his lifetime.

As I put the information into my phone, I follow the directions to where it tells me to turn left, but I don't see a road. Slowing down, I go to turn and see where the tall grasses separate. Taking a chance, I move forward and see where other vehicles have gone down. Downshifting, I continue forward until the tree cover starts to separate. It's dark under the cover of trees with peeks of lights shifting in. As the dirt road curves the trees open up and, holy fuck, in front of me is a bunch of buildings. Not old but definitely not new either. As I continue, that's when I see a bunch of trucks off to the side.

Before I even come to a stop, Coma walks over to the truck. I open the door and he waits 'til I'm on the ground.

"Brace, brother, this shit is beyond deranged. Seen and done a lot but this even shocked me. Nova is trying to take care of something, so he told me to show you what we found so far."

"Coma, I drove like a maniac for you to show me around a deserted bunch of buildings in the middle of bumfuck nowhere? Come on, man, life is knocking my ass down and this won't be helping, that's for sure."

"Who said this place is deserted, Yoggie? Come on, I'll show you what I'm talking about. We're waiting on one of Tink's transport trucks so we can start moving people out. Yeah, dude, I said people."

Following Coma through a door, the smell hits me first. A mix between body smells, exertion, and something I can't make out. The first room we come to there is probably five or so adults cowering in the corner, hanging on to each other. They are wearing rags and the smell is worse as you walk into the room. One of Nova's people is in there so we don't stop but continue forward. Each room has multiple people or children in it. We move to the next building, which is housing young men all chained to the wall. God only knows how long they've been here; they are skin and bone. As I'm scanning, one of the males is eyeballing me. I stop and he drops his head.

"Coma, have someone grab that one right there. Something is off with him. Put him to the side, don't let him go on the way out of here. I'll explain later."

As we continue forward, I'm appalled at what I'm seeing. How can someone do this to fellow human beings? How these folks will be able to move on from this is hard to even imagine. As we move from building to building, people are begging or screaming and crying. That is until I see, standing in the corner by herself, a young girl, arms crossed over her chest, head down, leaning up against the wall. Something about her catches my eye. Instead of following Coma, I walk toward her, though she doesn't lift her head at all. When I'm standing in front of her, she turns to the wall.

"Hey, my name is Yoggie. We're here to get you out of here, sweetie. Can I ask your name?"

I hear her let out a small sigh. What the hell, does the girl have a handicap? Maybe she is autistic like Teddy. I don't know. Then she whispers her name.

"My mom calls me Angel. The mean man calls me the little bitch and the other men call me mini tease."

What the fuck? This poor child has been emotionally, verbally, and not sure if physically abused. Her words are killing me. Then she slowly turns around and I feel my mouth drop and then my stomach shifts. I can't even comprehend what I'm seeing. Stepping back, I try to understand what—no, who—is right in front of me.

When I hear Coma come back to get me, he looks over my shoulder and I hear, "Holy mother of fucking shit." I look over my shoulder and he shuts up.

"Angel, do you know where your mother is? Is she here with you?"

"I don't know for sure. I see her every day but the jerk won't let us sleep in the same room. My mom said to just behave, stay quiet, and she'll figure a way for us to get free. Are you here to let us go? Are we free?"

Kneeling down in front of her, I leave my hands at my sides.

"Angel, I'm not sure, but I might know your grandma. You look like her. Would you be okay if I lift you and carry you out of here?"

She seems to study me for a while. When she steps forward, I don't move or barely breathe. Angel looks over my shoulder then back at me.

"You can carry me, but not him. Does he know my grandma too? And yes, please, Yoggie, you can take me out of here."

I pick her up, trying to ignore the smell coming from her. Poor child, even if she's not Nora's granddaughter we will do everything we can to help her move forward. As we walk through the door to the outside, Angel takes in a huge breath of air with her mouth open. Then her head falls backward and she puts her arms out like she doesn't have a care in the world. Just when I go to pull her back in, I hear a growl. As I go to turn around, Angel starts yelling.

"Mom, look, I'm outside. Yoggie and that man are

here to let us go free. Finally, Mom, we're free. What's wrong, you look mad? I'm sorry, Mom, I just wanted to be outside. I can't remember the last time we were allowed to come out here."

"I don't know who you are, asshole, but put my daughter down now. You will not touch her, the agreement is that you leave her alone and I'll do whatever you want, no questions. Come here, my Angel, come to Momma."

Turning slowly, I go to put Angel down, who instantly takes off running toward a woman in the doorway. When she steps off the stair to grab Angel, I know life as we know it is over. I can't believe my eyes. Coma is swearing like crazy as I see Nova standing behind the woman watching my face. When he gently eases by her and walks my way, all I can do is stare at the woman.

"What the hell are you staring at, mister? Sorry, Angel, Momma said a bad word. Don't use that word."

"Okay, Mom, I won't. What's next, Mom? Are we leaving or staying? I don't want to stay. Please, can we go?"

Angel's mom looks at her daughter then directly at me. Again, she asks the question of why I am staring at her. This time I answer.

"Well, I think I know your mom. No, give me a minute. You're Lilly and your mom is Norabelle or as we all know her as Nora. Right?"

THIRTY-THREE
'GLORY'
NORA

Trying to get dinner together, I'm surprised when Taz shows up to drop Olivia off. I thought Sebastian was picking her up after he visited with Tank. Something must have come up. He's been busting his ass with his club with the president down.

"Taz, you want a glass of wine? I'm having one, been a hell of a week. And that one right there is having some troubles. Hey, Olivia, go wash up then you can help me with dinner. Thanks, beauty."

Watching my girl head off to the bathroom, I turn to my sister, looking for her sidekick.

"Where's Teddy, Taz? Can't remember when I haven't seen the two of you together."

"Teddy went with Travis, who was taking Tuna to the vet again. Her bloodwork came back off and she's not feeling good, I can tell. Think she's lost some weight, so better safe than sorry. Yeah, I'll take a small glass of wine, if you don't mind. Where's Yoggie?"

"Working late again. He's really trying to help keep the Intruders running, I'm sure, just like Enforcer. Momma Diane told me Tank is chomping at the bit to get back to work. I hope soon we can get back to our crazy normal instead of whatever this is. Yoggie said Sheriff George is now working with a special unit that Nova hooked him up with that is working exclusively to end the Thunder Cloud Knuckle Brotherhood. Seems like they have been slowly breaking up different branches, I guess you'd call it. Some of those who are being arrested are people in power. Police, politicians, business owners, along with doctors, teachers, and even judges. So, seems like we might get our wish sooner rather than later."

Olivia comes skipping out, pulling her step stool over to help me with dinner. Tonight, we are having pasta with homemade meatballs. I'm working on making a salad and garlic bread. Taz takes over the bread while Olivia and I start getting the vegetables cut up for the salad. We are having a good time laughing and giggling. Olivia has us in stitches with antics that are all Teddy and Olivia. *Puppy love is so refreshing*, I think to myself.

I hear a phone ringing and watch Taz pick up her cell and answer it. She turns and walks to the family room, now whispering. When she looks over her shoulder and sees me watching her, she gives me a smile. Something is definitely up. She hangs up and comes back to where we are finishing up the salad.

"Well, Tuna's blood work is worse than we thought. Damn it, give me a minute."

She turns and I see her shoulders start to shake. *Oh no,* I think as I move to her side. Olivia watches and does the same thing but walks to her other side. I give her time.

"Sorry, sister. Travis said the vet is almost positive Tuna has lymphoma. I don't know what's next, but Teddy already told Travis we are doing whatever it takes because we aren't quitters. Then he busted out crying, so Travis is trying to console him. I need a break for something good to happen to us, Glory. It can't always be bad, can it?"

As we sit on the sectional, Taz and I with our wine and Olivia with her kiddie cocktail in a wine glass, we try to get back to our laughing and giggling. I can tell Taz is worried but for some reason she's not leaving. I hear a couple of bikes pull up and before I can even reach the door, I see Tink, Shadow, and Wildcat walking in the front door.

"What's up? Something going on? Come on in, anyone want some wine or a beer? Sebastian always keeps some on hand."

They go to sit in the family room just as I hear a car door slam. Then Raven, Vixen, and Rebel walk in. Damn, Vixen is starting to show. They just walk in and plop down at the kitchen table. What the fuck is going on? Before I can ask, in walks Hannah, Dottie, Dani, and Kitty.

"Okay, what the heck is going on? Are we having a

meeting at my house tonight and someone forgot to tell me? Who the hell is that now?'

Turning I see Duchess, Heartbreaker, Peanut, and finally Kiwi. These sisters walk around and take a seat on the floor facing toward me. That's it, but again someone beats me to it. And of course it's smart-mouthed Raven.

"Now, before you lose that temper of yours, we were told by Yoggie to get our asses here and wait 'til he gets here. All he said. So, cover that child's ears. Can you hear me, Olivia? Okay, so either you gave a one in a million blow job last night, or he's fallen captive to your woman garden. Maybe there's a ring involved. Y'all are dropping like flies."

By the time she's finished everyone is laughing. Well, guess I'll wait, though I always thought Sebastian would propose in private. Shared just between the two of us. As we all sit back and visit Olivia leans into me, trying to get comfortable. I see Taz texting back and forth. She's wiping her eyes so it's not good news about Tuna. So involved with everyone and what's going on, I miss the truck pulling up.

When the door swings open, I turn to see Yoggie walking in. He's got the strangest look on his face. He walks directly to me, grabbing my hands, pulling me up. Fuck, he's freaking me out. As he pulls me out of the family room into the kitchen area, I can hear everyone standing up and shifting here and there.

"Sebastian, what's going on? You look strange, like you've seen a ghost."

"Bae, do you trust me? I mean down to the root of your soul?"

Now I'm getting really nervous, maybe my sisters were right. Could he be getting ready to propose? Oh my God, and I look a mess, been running around all day. Shit. I look up and he's watching me with those gorgeous sapphire eyes.

"Sebastian, of course I trust you. Always and forever."

He drops his head, pulling me into him. I let him as he seems to be struggling with something. When he kisses the top of my head it's like he's come to a decision. He turns and grabs my hand, then puts his other out for Olivia. She goes to grab it and he changes his mind and picks her up while putting his arm around my waist.

Looking around, every single sister is on her feet waiting for me to pass. As I do, they all fall in line behind me. Damn, don't know if I can take much more. Olivia looks at me smiling, though I know she doesn't know what's going on. When Sebastian opens the door, I see all my sisters' men standing in our front yard. With them are most of the Intruders and, shit, Tank and Momma Diane are sitting on the porch in our rockers. What catches my eyes though is the huge black SUV. As soon as we get down off the porch, the front doors open and Nova steps out, along with Mayhem.

As they approach us, I watch the eye contact between Nova and Yoggie. Mayhem comes close and when Olivia sees him she squeals then motions for Yoggie to take her to Mayhem. The big guy has a way with the little ones.

"Evening, Glory. How ya doing?"

"Nova, was doing okay. Now I need to know what's going on. I know you two, no, three are in cahoots so just tell me. This is driving me insane. Just tell me, you're starting to piss me off."

I hear from a distance, "Mom, you said a bad word again."

"Glory, this is gonna be a total shock. Need you to take a seat. Yeah, right behind you. No, just relax, woman. Now, as you know, or probably know we've been busy trying to disband the brotherhood. Well, we came across something today, so yeah, Yoggie, we might as well just do it."

Sebastian stands behind me as Nova walks to the SUV, reaching for the passenger back door. He opens it and I can see there are people in there, don't know who. As they start moving, I can make out one young adult and the other looks to be a kid, maybe close to Olivia's age. A young woman steps out and immediately reaches for the kid. The woman hesitates with the child, I can see it's a girl in her arms.

I see her start to turn and I have a weird feeling start to run through my body. The more she turns the more I feel like electricity is running through me. When she's facing me, she lifts her head and I jump up off the chair so hard I hear Sebastian groan. The woman in front of me could be my twin or, holy mother of God, my daughter. I don't move and neither does she. Leave it to a child, what do they say, out of the mouths of babes.

"Are you my grandma? He said he knew her, is that you? You and mom look alike."

Before I know it, I'm running toward them just as the woman puts the little girl down.

"Lilly? Is that you, my beautiful daughter? My God, is this really happening? Are you my Lilly?'

The woman is staring at me then slowly smiles.

"Hey, Momma, yeah, I'm your Lilly."

We fall into each other's arms crying, laughing, screaming, and everything else in between. As we continue to hang on to each other, Sebastian comes to stand next to me with both Olivia and the little girl, who when I look at her, I can tell she's Lilly's.

"Momma, this is my daughter, Angel. Angel, this is your grandma."

The little girl leans toward me so I take her in my arms at the same time she gives me a little kiss on the cheek. I've died and gone to Heaven. I never want to lose this feeling for as long as I'm alive.

THIRTY-FOUR
'YOGGIE'
SEBASTIAN

The house is still quiet, which is a miracle. Since Lilly and Angel joined us, I'm now surrounded by four females. And I totally love it. It feels so right. Starting the coffee, I grab a cup and move to the front porch to sit on a rocker and enjoy the morning. I'm going to need to talk to Nora. If Lilly and Angel are planning on staying here, we'll need to build on because they'll need their own space. Right now, the two girls are sharing a room. Olivia and Angel are best friends, or besties, as they call it. Poor little Teddy is lost. It's not just him and Olivia but also Angel because the two girls are attached at the hip.

Hearing the screen door open, I assume it's Nora but when I look up, it's Lilly. It's taken some time to get used to seeing her because she does look so much like her mother. I wait because Lilly isn't a morning person, so I'm kinda shocked to see her up. After a couple of sips of her coffee, in her humongous coffee cup, she looks my way.

"Good morning, Sebastian. What's got you up so early sitting on the front porch?"

I smile at her, sarcasm this early is something for her. Guess therapy is helping because the first couple of weeks were brutal. Lilly thought everyone except Nora was out to get her. Yeah, rough. We've gotten through most of that.

"Morning, Lilly. Feeling your oats, are ya? I usually wake up early and grab coffee so I can start my day grateful and remember how very lucky I am to be alive."

I watch as she gets a smirk on her face, but then she looks at me and must see something.

"Why, Sebastian, are you lucky and grateful?"

Guess now is better than later. I spoke to the therapist and she said to share when I thought the timing was right. Well, we'll see.

"Lilly, when I was in the military, I was a prisoner of war for over eighteen months. So, I do understand a lot of what you're going through. I was treated like trash each and every day. I almost died twice because they tore parts of me that shouldn't have been torn. It's taken me many years to even talk about it."

"How did you manage to get out and keep living? Can I tell you something? I know I can trust you. I've had thoughts about killing myself, don't tell Mom. I'm talking to my therapist and Joan has put me on some medication. She told me it would take time and to get a schedule and follow it. So tomorrow, no sorry, today I'm going to talk to Tink to see if there is something I can do on her ranch. Maybe with the animals because I'm not liking being around people I don't know. And as soon as I can, Angel and I will be out of your hair."

"Lilly, no, you don't have to leave. You're not in my hair. Actually, I was gonna talk to you and your mom about maybe adding on so you and Angel could have your own space. Don't run out at my expense. I love having the two of you here. So drop that for now, 'kay?"

She goes to say something and stops as the door opens again, and my Bae comes out smiling. She grabs the lawn chair we keep up for when we are all out here, but I grab her hand and pull her onto my lap. Another thing Lilly is going to need to see is a normal relationship. Something she's never been exposed to since she was a young girl and saw her parents, before her nightmare began.

"So, what were you two talking about before I walked out? Looked pretty intense for this time in the morning. How's everyone doing? What's on your agendas today?"

I pull her into me, kissing her softly. When I pull away, she's looking a bit more relaxed. I hear Lilly and when I look, she's wiping tears away. Goddamn it.

"No, Sebastian, these are happy tears. I'm beyond thrilled that my mom has you in her life. Something both Angel and I need to see after what we've been through. I don't want my daughter to never experience real love. So please be you, never change that because it's a rare gift. Now, Mom, I was telling Sebastian that maybe Angel and I should move. Now wait, calm down, woman. He set me straight, so don't be surprised when the house starts to grow. Saying that, I'm going to get another cup of coffee. I can never thank you guys enough for all your doing for us. It truly means the world to me."

I feel Nora tremble with emotion as Lilly walks by. When she goes into the house, I feel my Bae let loose 'cause she starts to cry. I hold her throughout until she calms down and leans into me.

"Sebastian, thank you for being you. I doubt I ever would have made that first move so I'll never let you forget that you started this thing, and I can promise I'll never end it. I love you, Sebastian. You're my Yoggie bear."

"And you, Nora, are and always will be my Bae. Now let's get to talking about the addition we're going to have to build, so everyone has their own space."

When she pulls me to her, I go willingly. There is nowhere else I would rather be than on our porch with Nora on my lap and my lips on hers. Perfection. We've finally both found what we'd been looking for.

Forever and always.

* * *

***Want more Glory and Yoggie go to* https://dl.**

bookfunnel.com/pirmxw5gze *to download a bonus chapter.*

* * *

Check out the sneak peek of Raven, Book #6 on the next page.

RAVEN, SNEAK PEEK
'RAVEN'
BRENNA

It's been almost two weeks since I saw Ash's dumb as fuck brother at the hospital. Well, not actually that stupid 'cause he's one of Tank's doctors, but still my body trembles just thinking about his name. Since then I can't get him outta of my mind, which isn't good for me because the last time he just up and disappeared on me. It nearly broke me and if not for my brothers, sisters, and parents I'd probably have ended it all. Actually, Mom made me go speak to that therapist in Bozeman, which in the long run helped.

What hurts the most are the memories on video running through my mind day and night. I thought I'd finally put it all to rest, then I saw Reed out of the clear blue sky. Knowing sleep will not happen tonight, I get up and throw on my ratty-ass sweatshirt from a college. It hits me it's Ash's sweatshirt, but I can't part with it. Everything else I got rid of, except for a few boxes still in my parents' basement. I make my way to the kitchen, grab a coffee pod, and start my Keurig up.

While I wait, I go to the fridge, grab my oats creamer, and smile. God, would he love this creamer. Milk never agreed with him so he started drinking his coffee black, which he hated, especially since his family has one of the largest dairy farms in Montana. It was his dream to take over the family business after his dad retired. None of his brothers wanted it and he loved the land. Reed obviously became a doctor; Rue is on the rodeo circuit. Alder is working as a ranger for the state of Montana. Rowan, the baby, is still at home from what I hear. And the little I know from my mom, Ash is still on the farm doing what he does best, following his daddy's orders.

Grabbing my coffee, I put in my creamer then head to the front porch of my cabin. Tink was gracious enough to make sure all of the Devil's Handmaidens officers had the opportunity of having their own home. It also makes it easier for us to be close by if needed. Over the last few years it's been the best idea she ever came up with. For Christ's sake, my club sisters really can find them: the men in their lives and total drama.

Pushing back and forth on my porch swing, I think back on our dramas from Tink to, holy shit, Shadow, didn't know that sister had an emotion in her entire body. Well, until Panther came along. Damn, she hit the jackpot, though Tink's Noodles is no slouch. Biggest surprise was my hippy sister, Taz, putting her star on an Intruder and that brother being Intruder. Talk about badass though, all I ever see when he looks at Taz is true love. Vixen I relate to, as she found her one and only when she wrestled with her past. Ironside, the ex-FBI agent, had a rough go, not only with Vixen but all of us because we all knew how badly she was hurt when he all but disappeared on her. Finally, Glory and another Intruder, this time a prospect, Yoggie. Damn, I moved too slow on that one. My mind draws up that memory of walking in Glory's room to find that fine as fuck specimen of a man lying in her bed. In the end though, each of my sisters is happy and that makes me happy. I'm still lonely and alone and that doesn't make me content.

Trying to blank my mind of everything, I still, swing, and watch the sun start to rise. It surprises me that, even being a night person, I love watching the sun come up. Especially like today when the ranch is quiet since everyone is probably still asleep. I can barely hear the horses whinny and some moos from our cows. Someone has let a dog out 'cause I can hear them barking. Ranch life is truly the best. And being a Devil's Handmaiden sister comes in a close second.

Seeing a truck make its way up the long-ass driveway has the hair on the back of my neck go up. At this time in the morning, who the hell could this be? I know that between Tank and Tink the gate is guarded at all times, so whoever it is had to pass through that checkpoint. I see the truck pass the main house and swing around to the cabins. Well, which sister is expecting an early morning guest or maybe a booty call? Can't wait to see where the pickup stops so I can have some juicy news. I can then make one of my sister's crazy as I think up all kinds of funny shit.

So stuck in my own thoughts of fucking with a sister, it takes me a second or two to notice the truck stopped in front of my cabin. Who the hell is it? *One of my brothers*, I think, though I don't recognize the brand-new Chevy Silverado parked in front of me. Trying to squint to see who it is, the sun isn't helping, so I lean forward and wait. Apparently, whoever is in the truck is doing the exact same thing.

When the door opens, I've convinced myself it has to be one of my brothers because who else would come out this early. Unless maybe it's Onyx. Now that she's part of the Blue Sky Sanctuary I've seen her around a lot. She's trying to repair our relationship, and so am I. I miss my sister.

Hearing the door slam, I look and I feel for Tank as I feel like I'm having a goddamn heart attack. Never in a million years would I think it was him. Gave up on that when he dumped me during our engagement party at my folks' house. Yeah, we were young as shit. I was what—seventeen, no, maybe eighteen—and madly in love with this asinine jerk. Never taking my eyes from him, he makes his way to and up the stairs. When he's in front of me, the cowboy hat comes off and he hangs on to it with his fingers, which are turning white. This is his rodeo not mine, so I sit back and wait.

"Morning, darlin'. Ya ain't gonna make this easy on me, are ya? Told Reed nothin' had changed but he swore you were different. Guess he's an idiot wearing a doctor's coat. I came here to try and make peace, Brenna. Is that even possible? Can you give me a chance to explain?"

Taking time I try to keep my temper in. First, I try to count to ten then twenty and finally fifty. No, it isn't working, damn it. Closing my eyes, I take in a couple of deep breaths like Taz is always telling us to do when stressed out. Now that worked, so I do it again. Okay, I can do this. Until I opened my eyes and Ash is standing right in front of me. Dang it, he can still move like a bobcat. He almost scared the crap out of me.

"Still move like a wild bobcat, don't you? What do you want, Ash, I got shit to do?"

"Told you, want to make peace between us. Since that day our families are torn apart and it's our fault. My mom and dad miss your parents, and I'm sure they miss my parents too. My brothers haven't been hunting with your brothers since then. We need to fix this, darlin'. So I'm being a gentleman, coming to you to try and figure out how to do it."

Feeling my head getting ready to blow off my shoulders, I stand up so fast the swing moves back and then hits me in the ass and upper thighs, sending me straight into Ash's arms. For Christ's sake, I can't make this shit up. He grabs my upper arms, holding me until I catch my balance.

"Get your hands off me, Ash, you lost that privilege a long time ago. And as far as making peace, a good way to start is to tell me why you dumped me in the middle of our GODDAMN ENGAGEMENT PARTY you asshole. Then you took off with Patsy Woods. How do you think that made me feel, you dickless jerk?"

He has the decency to drop his head down, but as usual says nothing. I'm done, so I move past him, going to the door. Before I can push it open, he's in front of me, blocking my way. Oh no, not playing any games. I shift and when I lift my leg to knee him in the groin; he moves faster than me. In the next minute I'm up against the cabin and his entire body is plastered behind me. I can feel how huge he's gotten, and I mean huge everywhere. His breath is on my neck before I feel his lips there. Holy shit, no. I don't want this, swore to never forgive him for what he did and put me through.

I try to push him off but he's too strong. Then I throw my head back and hear an 'oof' but he doesn't let go. When he leans into me again, I can feel something wet dripping on my neck so must have gotten him in the nose. Good for me.

"Darlin', enough of this bullshit. We need to have a grown-up conversation. Yeah, I know, Brenna, something you're not used to but ya need to hear me out. So is that gonna happen today or do I need to keep coming here 'cause I don't have a problem with that. One way or another we are gonna talk, you tell me when."

Before I can say a word, I hear a growl right before Ash is yanked away. When I turn I see Avalanche wailing on him. Fuck, Shadow's Big Bird is going to kill my Ash. Wait he isn't mine anymore.

"Avalanche, no, please let him up. Shit, brother,

you're going to kill him and he isn't worth it. Avalanche, please."

He looks up at me then down at Ash, whose face is already swelling. Avalanche drops his head, all that beautiful hair of his covering his face. Then he lets Ash go and stands up. When he offers Ash his hand, my heart wishes I could fall for Avalanche. He's one in a million.

"Raven, what the hell is going on? I come back here to do a walk by and see this asshole, well dude, has you pushed up against the cabin. Oh shit, did I interrupt a sexual moment? Are you into what do they call it yeah voyeurism? Oh fuck, didn't mean to intrude, you two. I can get outta of your hair. Sorry, man, not my intention at all."

"Avalanche, shut the hell up. No, you didn't interrupt a tryst at all. And no I don't like people to see me having sex for Christ's sake. This is my ex, who suddenly decided we need to make nice. Don't know why, but that's what he's trying to sell to me. As I told Ash, I'm not buying it, but he won't take no for an answer. As you can see by his bloody nose, I tried to explain it first vocally then physically. That's where we are right now."

Ash has been watching the interaction between Avalanche and me, and the look on his face shocks me. He actually looks hurt. What is that?

"Is he the reason we can't move on, Darlin'? Obviously you did…uhm, moved on. Good for you. Sorry to bother ya. Hope you both have a nice day. No wait, I actually hope it totally sucks cow balls. You have no idea how hard this was for me to come here, Brenna, and you treat me like a piece of shit on your boot. Was gonna try to explain and hoped you at least would listen, but no, not you. Well, you are getting what you wished for, I'm gone."

With that he stomps to his truck, turns it on, shifts, pulling out and leaving us in a dust and smoke. I'm in total shock and just stand here watching his truck drive away. I actually jump when Avalanche whistles.

"That motherfucker has it bad, Raven. Whatcha do to him back in the day? Almost feel sorry for the son of a bitch. Come on, tell your brother, what's going on?"

Instead of speaking I feel a breakdown coming. I try to make it up the porch and inside the cabin, but Avalanche grabs my arm and before he can pull me into him, the tears are already running down my face. Damn, there go my credentials as the clown. Nothing funny here, for sure.

"Come on, Raven, let's get inside and you can tell your big, handsome, studly brother all about it."

His words do exactly what he intended. I snort then giggle. We make it back into my cabin, with me still crying but also laughing. Damn, why doesn't fate work for me? I could be in bed with this stud instead of offering him some coffee. Oh well, welcome to my world.

Grab your copy of Raven, Book 6 now!

ABOUT THE AUTHOR

USA Today Bestselling author, D. M. Earl creates authentic and genuine characters while spinning stories that feel so real and relatable that the readers plunge deep within the plot, begging for more. Complete with drama, angst, romance, and passion, the stories jump off the page.

When Earl, an avid reader since childhood, isn't at her keyboard pouring her heart into her work, you'll find her in Northwest Indiana snuggling up to her husband, the love of her life, with her seven fur babies nearby. Her other passions include gardening and shockingly cruising around town on the back of her 2004 Harley. She's a woman of many talents and interests. Earl appreciates each and every reader who has ever given her a chance--and hopes to connect on social media with all of her readers.

Contact D.M at DM@DMEARL.COM
Website: http://www.dmearl.com/

facebook.com/DMEarlAuthorIndie
x.com/dmearl
instagram.com/dmearl14
amazon.com/D-M-Earl/e/B00M2HB12U
bookbub.com/authors/d-m-earl
goodreads.com/dmearl
pinterest.com/dauthor

ALSO BY D.M. EARL

DEVIL'S HANDMAIDENS MC SPINOFF
Running Wild

DEVIL'S HANDMAIDENS MC: TIMBER-GHOST, MONTANA CHAPTER
Tink (Book #1)

Shadow (Book #2)

Taz (Book #3)

Vixen (Book #4)

Glory (Book #5)

GRIMM WOLVES MC SERIES
Behemoth (Book 1)

Bottom of the Chains-Prospect (Book 2)

Santa…Nope The Grimm Wolves (Book 3)

Keeping Secrets-Prospect (Book 4)

A Tormented Man's Soul: Part One (Book 5)

Triad Resumption: Part Two (Book 6)

Fractured Hearts - Prospect (Book 7)

WHEELS & HOGS SERIES
Connelly's Horde (Book 1)

Cadence Reflection (Book 2)

Gabriel's Treasure (Book 3)

Holidays with the Horde (Book 4)

My Sugar (Book 5)

Daisy's Darkness (Book 6)

The Journals Trilogy

Anguish (Book 1)

Vengeance (Book 2)

Awakening (Book 3)

Stand Alone Titles

Survivor: A Salvation Society Novel

Printed in Great Britain
by Amazon